A MYSTERY SOLVED
A Prediction Fulfilled

A MYSTERY SOLVED
A Prediction Fulfilled

An Ellen Jones Novel
by Alayne Smith

Ellard
publishing

Lawrenceville, GA

A Mystery Solved, A Prediction Fulfilled
An Ellen Jones Novel

Ellard
publishing

Published by Ellard Publishing
Lawrenceville, GA

ISBN 978-1-7366448-3-6 paperback
ISBN 978-1-7366448-4-3 e-book

prologue

January 1, 1962

Sitting down on my bed, I reach for my baby book, buried in the bottom drawer of my bedside table. A sheet of paper flutters softly out of the baby book and falls at my feet.

There on the paper are Luella's predictions.

Luella is the local soothsayer who claims to have the eye to see the future. Even the learned citizens of Marshall, Alabama, go to Luella for predictions of their babies' lives.

I look down at her predictions for me. There are three:

She will be an advocate for the beauty.

She will foil a dictator.

She will find the soldier.

Chapter One
Ellen Jones

Thursday, March 8, 1962

"It's that mint julep cabinet. The carving in the cabinet gives a date for your great grandmother's marriage. The family Bible lists another date and a different groom altogether. It's driving me crazy." After the slightest pause, the voice on the other end of the line says, "When are you coming home for spring break to help me solve this mystery?"

Aunt Essie is calling long distance from Marshall, Alabama. Ellen heard the phone ring on her dorm floor at Columbus University, and, knowing no one else would answer, she picked it up to hear Aunt Essie—who has not stopped talking since Ellen picked up.

Essie is sister to Ellen's father, Will. After Ellen's mother died, Essie moved in with Ellen and Will. Actually, she did more than just move in. She saved the two of them. Essie fed their bodies and their souls during that terrible time after Ellen's mother died. Ellen loves Essie, in spite of her eccentricities—or perhaps because of them—and she has promised to help her solve the mystery of the mint julep cabinet. The marble-topped cabinet is where they keep the bourbon and the fancy glasses for occasions when they mix bourbon and sugar and pour it over ice and mint. Ugh!

"Essie, you know I'll be home Friday, the 16th. We'll have one full week to solve your mystery!"

"Fine. You know, child, I can hardly wait to see you."

"And me you, Aunt Essie."

"Let's have a feast and celebrate. Luke 15:23," says Essie. A smile breaks out on Ellen's face. She can't help it. Essie always closes a conversation with a Bible verse. It's just her way.

Ellen is a junior at Columbus University in Miami, majoring in broadcast journalism. Lately, she has been exploring her options in the broadcasting field. Does she want to be a reporter? A director? She's not sure. Probably not an anchor, though she's due in the broadcasting studio to anchor the college news show in fifteen minutes. Dr. Shelby, head of the department, is making sure Ellen experiences all broadcasting roles while she's here at Columbus.

***

"Sound check, Ellen," yells the audio technician from the control room. Ellen begins reading from the script in front of her on the broadcasting studio desk.

"Now you, Sandra."

Ellen watches Sandra as she performs a flawless sound check. This girl was her nemesis during first semester—always after Luke, Ellen's former boyfriend. Unfortunately, Sandra looks like a movie star with her cloud of dark hair and long fingernails, polished candy apple red.

When the sound checks are finished, Sandra turns to Ellen, confidently flipping her dark hair. "What do you hear from Luke? Oh, that's right. You *don't* hear from Luke, do you?" Before Ellen can respond, the floor director, his hands held high, counts down from five with his fingers. Reaching one, he signals for the anchors to go.

> Good evening and welcome to Miami News Now. I'm Sandra Rowen.
>
> And I'm Ellen Jones. Fallout shelters are a part of our world. In fact, an underground fallout shelter built for President Kennedy is situated just seventy-eight miles from here on Peanut Island. The U.S. Navy Seebees built the shelter over the course of a two-week period in December 1960, and it will house thirty people for thirty days.

> The shelter is covered with layers of dirt, concrete, and steel reinforcement bars and is entered through a tunnel. Inside are shelves stocked with gas masks, containers of drinking water, and food called K-rations, which does not need refrigeration.
>
> In the advent of a nuclear attack, President Kennedy could be moved by helicopter from Palm Beach to Peanut Island in five minutes.
>
> Sandra ...

Ellen thinks ahead to her next story as Sandra delivers a story about the use of Agent Orange in Vietnam.

***

Leaving the broadcasting building, or J building as it's often called, Ellen fumes over Sandra's snide remark about Luke. Luke was the one. He and Ellen were to be married, although they disagreed about whether she should finish her degree at Columbus first. Luke was a senior, and he had expected Ellen to give up her senior year of college to follow him. Then he cheated.

Ellen's Aunt Zia, a former reporter for CBS and a strong influence on her choice of a career path, had invited Luke to go with her when she interviewed two soldiers who were at the Bay of Pigs invasion. Zia had not yet published her story when Luke, using Zia's information, entered his own story in the Peabody Awards competition. Ellen instantly recognized the information in Luke's story. When Luke was expelled from the university, he lost any chance of marrying her.

It still hurt her to think of Luke, the handsome man who commanded the space around him. Luke the Legend—the man with the clear blue eyes who looked a little like Paul Newman. Luke's goal was to work in a major broadcasting market straight out of college, and the Peabody Award was a stepping stone to that goal. How very sad that Luke was expelled before he could finish his senior year.

The last Ellen knew of Luke, he was working in Atlanta for the local newspaper and looking for a university to accept him. He needed to finish his last semester if he had any hope of a career at all, much less a major market job.

Ellen can't help contrasting Luke to Jo Jo, the sharecropper's son she grew up with on her grandfather's plantation, Callander. There is a certain comfort being around someone who has known you all your life. Jo Jo and Ellen share so many high school memories, including a kiss in a field on Callander land with no one around and a magical prom night.

Out of high school, Jo Jo attended the Air Force Academy and is currently in the Air Force serving in Tripoli, Libya. Ellen has learned so much about Tripoli through his letters.

She loves reading them and seeing his predictable line, "You're still my girl," at the bottom of each letter. Even when she was with Luke, Ellen felt a pull toward Jo Jo. She wasn't sure what to make of it. Even now.

On her way to her dorm room at Caldwell Hall, Ellen stops by the campus post office. Entering the old door by turning the worn brass doorknob, she searches the lines of little wooden boxes with brass fronts, combination locks, and small windows to peek inside and see if you have mail. Ellen is delighted to see a blue envelope through her mailbox window. That means a letter from Jo Jo.

Removing the letter and walking outside to her favorite bench, she reads Jo Jo's letter.

Dear Ellen,

Tripoli is all astir. They are planning something called the Tripoli Fair Tournament which involves what they call football and we call soccer. You know how I love sports. This is a men's football event and will be held for the first time this year with Arab men playing against players from other countries like Great Britain and Tunisia. I think it's part of the Tripoli International Fair, which is a pretty big deal. Wish airmen could play.

Bill and Ilenia are planning a June wedding.
They will be married in Tripoli with Ilenia's dad
running the show. Ilenia has little input into her
own wedding and poor Bill has none. I do know
there will be a reception in the States, so Bill's
family and friends can attend. That will happen
in late June, after Bill is rotated to the States for
his next duty station.

Remember, I'll be home this summer. I am
counting the days 'til I see you. I imagine you
walking the fields at Callander, and it makes me
happy.

What if we could go to the wedding
together? We'll talk.

You're still my girl,

JoJo

Ellen kisses the letter and places it back in the envelope. She is happy for Bill and Ilenia. She remembers when she feared Ilenia and JoJo were a thing. How very fabulous to learn Ilenia loves Bill, Jo Jo's roommate on the base in Tripoli and a broadcast journalist like herself.

Lots of decisions lay ahead. What journalism career to pursue? Is JoJo the one? How will she know? But first, there's Aunt Essie and the mystery of the mint julep cabinet.

Chapter Two
Ellen Jones

Friday, March 16, 1962

Passing by the row of sharecroppers' cottages with tin roofs, porches with worn chairs, and smoke pouring from the single chimneys, Ellen knows she is home—back on Callander land. Callander, her grandfather's place consisting of 1,200 acres in total, is a working plantation with a grist mill, commissary, syrup mill, sawmill, blacksmith shop, and cotton gin. Her grandfather, Henry David Callander, lives in the plantation house with his daughter, Ellen's Aunt Zia, and her husband David.

Ellen emulates Zia and goes to her for advice and comfort when she needs it. When Zia was a reporter for CBS, she was assigned to produce a documentary on Batista in Cuba. While there for the story, Zia met and fell in love with David Foca. She married David and the two were living in Havana when Castro took over the country.

Zia and David were able to get David's son, Julio, out of Cuba through the Pedro Pan Movement, but David's daughter embraced Castro and died while participating in the Literacy Campaign. David and Zia, at separate times, were in La Cabaña, a fortress prison. Both were held for opposing Castro, and both had miraculously escaped and come home to Callander.

Ellen will see Zia at the plantation house in the morning, but now she is headed home to the four-bedroom brick home on Callander land to see her father, Will, and his wife, Amanda. Ellen looks at her childhood home fondly as she pulls up at the back door.

Before she can knock, Ellen is in her father's arms. She just lets go—of all the tensions in her life, of all the decisions to be made—and leans into her father's arms, loving his strength and soaking up the obvious love he has for her.

Ellen kisses Will on the cheek, then turns to Amanda. Her father's second wife has found a spot in Ellen's heart. Ellen loves her for willing her father to come to life again after the death of Ellen's mother.

Her father turned to her. "Ellen, we want you all to ourselves, but, if you don't get over to Essie's to see her about some cabinet, she's going to burst. I promised I'd send you over as soon as you unpacked."

"But Dad..."

"That's all right, Sug. Amanda and I have you for dinner. Amanda's cooking something special with a name I can't pronounce. You get settled and get to Essie's."

"Okay, Dad. I'll be back for dinner. Love you two."

***

Essie lives in just about the most fabulous house in Marshall. It is antebellum, built before the Civil War. The two-story home is painted white with black shutters and has four columns lined up across the front porch. The house, called the Mitchell House to this day, was built by Essie and Will's grandfather, Thomas Brown Mitchell.

Essie is waiting on the back porch when Ellen pulls up behind the house.

"Child, I thought you'd never get here. I'm so happy to see you."

"Well, I'm happy to see you, too," says Ellen, hugging Essie around what used to be an ample middle. Stepping back, Ellen notices that Aunt Essie has slimmed down, straightened her curly hair, and is wearing stylish shoes. *What's going on with this new Essie?* Ellen keeps her thoughts to herself for now.

"Come in. Come in. May I offer you some lemonade or tea or something?"

"No, I'm fine, Aunt Essie. Let's hear about your mint julep cabinet. Anything new?"

Talking as she walks to the front parlor, Essie says, "Oh, no. I've been waiting for you. Now, remember, the family Bible recorded your great-grandmother, Mary Ellen Davis, married Thomas Brown Mitchell in December of 1866."

"Yes, Aunt Essie, I remember, and the mint julep cabinet has great-grandmother marrying Thaddeus Baird in May of 1866, just seven months earlier." Hugging Essie again, Ellen says, "And we're going to solve the mystery and find out who Mary Ellen really married. Now, where do we start?"

"In the attic. I haven't been up there, because I have been waiting for you."

"Right, Aunt Essie. And, admit it, you don't want to go to the attic by yourself."

"Guilty, but I'm fine now. I've got you with me, so lead the way."

The attic is accessed through a door that leads out of the main bedroom and up wooden stairs covered in cobwebs. When Ellen and Essie reach the top of the stairs, they stop, amazed. The attic is filled with cast-off furniture, baby buggies, and trunks—tons of trunks—lined up along a center aisle. Standing out among all the cast-offs is a dress dummy outfitted in a beautiful dress, almost certainly a wedding dress with its lace trimmed bodice and long, flowing lace train.

"Look at this, Aunt Essie. I bet you it's a wedding dress. Wouldn't it be something if Mary Ellen was married in this white, lacy dress?"

"You know this business of wearing white at a wedding started when Queen Victoria married Albert and wore a white lace dress. That was in 1840. All the brides have been wearing white ever since—except me."

"Oh, Essie. You have to tell me about your wedding. And all about your dress. And about Uncle James. I don't remember him. Was he wonderful?"

"That is a story for another day. Right now, I suggest we tackle these trunks."

"I'll take the trunks on the left, and you take the trunks on the right. We'll open them all and cross your fingers we find more clues about Mary Ellen," says Ellen.

Essie and Ellen begin opening the trunks one at a time. "I swear, Ellen, I don't think anyone has been up here since after the Civil War. I should have thought to bring dust rags."

"We'll do that next time."

After what seems like hours, Ellen opens a small trunk. In the top tray, a stack of cards is nestled next to a stack of newspapers, moth-eaten and yellowed from the passage of time. Ellen unfolds the top article. The masthead reads *Marshall Times-Standard*, and Ellen immediately spots an article on the front page with a byline: Mary Ellen Davis.

"Essie, I may have found Mary Ellen. Come look." In her excitement, Ellen drops the article. Flustered, she picks it up and hands it to Essie.

"Oh, you *have* found her. Just look at this. An article on the Civil War dead left on the battlefield written by Mary Ellen Davis. Seek and you shall find. Matthew 7:7."

Ellen smiles at Essie's quirkiness. Looking at her watch, she is surprised to see it is almost six o'clock—dinnertime for Will and Amanda.

"Essie, I'm sorry to leave Mary Ellen when we've just found her, but, if I don't run, I'm going to be late for dinner with Amanda and Dad. I promise to be back right after lunch tomorrow."

"Don't worry, child. You are a saint for helping me, and I'll see you tomorrow."

"You can stay, Aunt Essie. There's so much to look through."

"Not on your life," says Essie, following Ellen down the attic stairs.

Reaching the bottom stair, Ellen turns to Essie. "I'm so excited, Aunt Essie. I can't wait to find out more about Mary Ellen Davis." The two walk together to the front entrance of Essie's grand home. The sun is just beginning its descent across the town of Marshall.

Chapter Three
Mary Ellen Davis

Wednesday, April 4, 1866

"Mary Ellen Davis, get down here this instant."

"Coming, Mama."

"Dinner is on the table. Stop writing those stories long enough to come eat."

Mary Ellen sighs and puts down her pen. She's trying to finish a story on the mayor of Marshall, Alabama, for the *Marshall Times-Standard*. Realizing how lucky she is to be able to work for the paper at the age of fifteen, Mary Ellen is determined to impress Mr. Hughes, owner of the *Times-Standard*. Licking her fingers, she smoothes her fly-away brown hair away from her temples and shakes out her skirts.

Walking toward the dining room, Mary Ellen can tell she's the last one at the table from the chatter she hears.

"Most young ladies are married by now. Mary Ellen just wants to write for that darn paper," her mother says.

"Now, Olivia. There's plenty time for Mary Ellen to marry. Leave her alone. She's a born journalist. Mr. Hughes told me so."

"You spoil her, Mason."

"So, I'm the topic of conversation?" says Mary Ellen, sitting down next to her brother, Adam.

"You're always the topic of conversation at Revival House," says Adam.

Before Mary Ellen can retort, Sara, a platter of fried squash in one hand and a bowl of black-eyed peas in the other, pushes the door into the dining room open with her back and heads toward the table. Sara winks at Mary Ellen as she puts the platter and bowl down on the dining room table. "Miss Mary Ellen, did you hear about that new school for our sharecropper kids? You might wanna write about it."

"I heard about it just this morning at the Methodist men's meeting. Thomas Mitchell has started a school for the sharecropper children in the kitchen behind the old Garvey plantation house," says Mary Ellen's father.

"Who's Thomas Mitchell? And is that all you get out of rubbing minds with the other men—just the local gossip?" says Mary Ellen's mother.

Patting his wife's hand, Mary Ellen's father turns to Mary Ellen, "Thomas Mitchell was just a child when the Civil War started. Nonetheless, he fought bravely at the Battles of Mobile Bay and Fort Blakeley. Was wounded at

Fort Blakeley. Had his knee blown out with a musket ball. This morning, I heard he was spending his time teaching the young sharecropper children to read and write. A noble venture."

"Sara, thank you for telling me about Mr. Mitchell. I think it's a good story for the *Times-Standard*, and I'll talk to Mr. Hughes about it," says Mary Ellen.

"Humph!" says Mary Ellen's mother.

"Now, Mother, leave the girl alone," says Mary Ellen's father. "Listen up now; I have some news. My college roommate's son will be in Marion for the summer, taking a class at Howard College. Sara, I want you to prepare something special this weekend. Thaddeus is coming to lunch here at Revival House."

"Well, how nice he is at Howard College, near us. I think fried chicken will do, Sara," says Mary Ellen's mother.

Ever the reporter, Mary Ellen asks, "Why Howard and why the summer?"

"I understand from Thaddeus' father that Thaddeus wants to teach at the University of Alabama. Hugh thinks it would be excellent for Thaddeus' curriculum vitae to have studied under Professor A.B. Goodhue. Goodhue has made a name for himself in the field of education by continuing to teach at Howard during the Civil War, including teaching wounded soldiers in the hospital. You remember Howard was a hospital for Confederate soldiers from '63 right up to last year."

"Well, Revival House will open its doors to this young man. And, Mary Ellen, maybe he'll be interested in a lady who enjoys writing as a pastime." Mary Ellen looks at Adam and crosses her eyes. Adam's laugh earns a scowl from his mother.

***

"I swear, Adam. I'd look forward to leaving here one day, if I didn't love Revival House so much."

"Aw, Doodle, don't talk that way," says Adam. Adam's nickname for Mary Ellen has been Doodle most of her life. Adam came up with the nickname because, even as a child, Mary Ellen was writing. Writing stories about the cat. Or Sara's fried okra. Or Christmas at Revival House.

Revival House was built by Mary Ellen's grandfather in the early 1800s, and it is the only home Mary Ellen has known. A Greek Revival cottage with ornate columns marching across the front porch, the wide double-front doors of Revival House are topped with a transom, and small windows line up in a vertical pattern on both sides of the door.

Coming in the front door, there's a wide hall, like the ones found in so many homes built in the 1800s, and two high-ceiling rooms on each side of the hallway. The two rooms to the left are a gentleman's parlor with a dining room behind it. The room to the right is a ladies' parlor with the master bedroom behind it. Off the back of the house is a porch with a kitchen and two bedrooms jutting off the porch, but the main attraction is the ballroom. Even the word is so romantic. *Ballroom!*

Mary Ellen's grandfather added a wing to the west of the house for the sole purpose of entertaining, and Mary Ellen's parents follow the tradition. Revival House is always on the Marshall Tour of Homes. For the duration of the event, the entire family is scattered in various rooms around the house, each with a prepared speech. Mary Ellen is always stationed in the ballroom, her favorite, full speech prepared:

"Welcome to the ballroom, the most spectacular room in the house. Notice the four ceiling-to-floor windows on each side of the room. Stepping back from the windows, observe three fluted columns marching down each side of the room. You just *have* to notice the twelve-foot ceiling, which is shorter than the fourteen-foot ceilings in the rest of the house. While glancing up, don't forget to look at the rose-shaped plaster medallions with crystal chandeliers hanging from the centers. Just close your eyes and imagine beautifully gowned women and men in coats with tails dancing the Minuet."

To this day, Revival House is known for late suppers with dancing, and romantic Mary Ellen loves the very idea of dancing in the family ballroom. No, she was in no hurry

to marry off and move away. It would be very hard to leave
Revival House.

Chapter Four
Ellen Jones

Saturday, March 17, 1962

At the Callander plantation house, Zia and Ellen catch up over breakfast. Lila, who has cooked for David Henry Callander longer than anyone can remember, makes the best biscuits in Alabama. Slicing one so she can add butter and muscadine preserves, Ellen asks, "How are you and David adjusting to life at Callander?"

"It's been less than three months. David and I are still getting used to the idea that we are here together. For a long time, I thought he'd never be able to leave Cuba."

"And he is still mourning Carlota," Ellen said softly. "Even as young as I am, I cannot imagine the horror of losing a child."

"I tell you, Ellen, it's horrible. I wake up during the night, and David is not in bed. He's out on the front porch in one of the rockers, crying. I know he is crying for Carlota, but I think he is crying for Cuba as well."

"But Aunt Zia, you know the Callander folks are going to embrace him. This will be his home now."

"Of course. Being at Callander, with its warm-blanket feeling, is so comforting. But David is a man of action. He won't stand in this one place long."

"Do you have any idea what he's thinking?"

"He mentioned contacting an old friend in New Orleans. You know, after he graduated from Columbia, he spent a year in New Orleans working in sugar refineries. That's the only thing he's mentioned to me that even smacks of moving on. And, speaking of moving on, have you completely divorced yourself from Luke?"

"Of course I have. How could I ever have a relationship with him after what he did—stealing your story?"

"Luke called me, you know."

"No, I don't know. When?"

"Back in January. He is working at the *Atlanta Journal*, writing hard news stories. He indicated the *Journal* would recommend him to the broadcasting program at the University of Alabama, if he worked for them for one year."

"I think he is getting off easy."

"Don't be so hard on him, Ellen. I respect him for calling me to apologize. And you are judging, Ellen. If Aunt Essie were here, she would say, 'Do not judge, or you too will be judged. For in the same way you judge others, you will be judged. Matthew 7:1.'"

Ellen puts a hand over her mouth to hold back peals of laughter. It doesn't work. She laughs out loud. "You are so right about Aunt Essie. I deserve that. But, my gosh Aunt Zia, I was going to marry Luke. I hurt. And I hurt for him."

"He gave me a message for you, Ellen."

"He did?"

"He said tell Cotton I am sorry I messed everything up. That's what hurts the most, losing her."

"You know, Aunt Zia, maybe he will make it to that major market station he wants so badly. I'll try my best about this judging business."

"Good. Now, let's talk about the other man in your life."

"Jo Jo?"

"Is there any other man in your life?"

"You know there's not. Jo Jo writes me from Tripoli. Funny, he usually ends his letters with 'You're still my girl.'"

"And are you?"

"I think so, Aunt Zia, but I'm not positive. We've been away from each other for a long time. He's coming home this summer. I think I'll know for sure then."

Standing up, Zia walks behind Ellen. Leaning down, she kisses her niece on the top of her head. "My smart, honest girl. I think you'll figure it out just fine. Now, I think you'd better get to Essie's. You know she's waiting for you. Probably not very patiently."

***

Once again, Essie is waiting for Ellen on the back porch. She speaks so fast Ellen can hardly understand her, Essie says, "You are here. I'm so excited." Grabbing Ellen by the hand, Essie leads her up the staircase, talking just as fast as she walks. "We know Mary Ellen wrote for newspapers. Do you think it's in your genes? Writing, I mean."

"I always thought Aunt Zia inspired me, but it's a nice thought. I'd like to think it's in my genes."

Essie looks around the attic, spots the small trunk with Mary Ellen's newspaper articles in it, and sees the furniture stacked up behind both rows of trunks. "Let's each find something to sit on. Then we can go through the small trunk together."

"Good idea, Aunt Essie." Ellen finds a cushioned stool and drags it over to the small trunk. She ignores the stack of articles and cards in the top tray, lifts the tray, and puts it aside.

"Oh, Essie, look." Ellen holds in her hands an old book with pictures pasted inside on the heavy, yellowed paper. A photograph of a striking woman seated in a tufted-back armchair catches her eye. A tall, distinguished man stands behind her, a girl of maybe ten or eleven to one side, and a younger boy to the other. Written in ink below the picture:

Mason and Olivia Davis with children,
Mary Ellen and Adam.

The year 1850.

"Let's make a stack of things I can take downstairs to go through later. Do you want to add the book to the pile?" says Essie.

"Sure. Look at this, Aunt Essie." Ellen gingerly lifts what appears to be a ballgown out of the chest. It is the palest blue taffeta with an off-the-shoulder top and a full skirt that probably touched the floor in a whisper.

Reaching in, Essie says, "And this. Do you know what this is?" Essie is holding a small leather book with a tiny pencil attached. Inside, eighteen dances, including waltzes and polkas, are listed with a space beside each. A gentleman's name is written in the space beside each dance.

"I've heard about them. It's a dance card, right? And look, Mary Ellen's card is full."

"Look at the last name on the card: Thaddeus Baird."

"Oh, Essie. Mary Ellen wore this dress and danced with Thaddeus Baird. Don't you have chills?"

"I certainly do."

Digging down below the dress, Ellen finds a quilt and tissue-wrapped packets. She opens a few and finds napkins and pillowcases made of linen and lace, trimmed with tiny embroidered flowers.

"You are probably looking at Mary Ellen's trousseau."

"What is that, Aunt Essie?"

"All young women in Mary Ellen's time had hope chests or trousseaus, which they filled with items they were saving for marriage. So, *hope chest*— hope to marry."

"Do you feel close to Mary Ellen? I do."

"Yes, I understand what you mean. This closeness. Like we are seeing a piece of her life."

"Yes. Exactly." Ellen picks up the tray and places it in the trunk. Then she looks at the cards. We can add the newspaper articles and cards in your pile to take downstairs, but I have to look at least one of these cards."

Ellen opens the top envelope. It is a note, seemingly from a child, written to Miss Davis. It reads:

May 11, 1866
Jericho School

Dear Miss Davis,

Thank you for working with us on Fridays.

I love that we both like to write.

Respectively,
Benjamin

"Based on finding the newspaper articles in this same trunk, this has to be our Mary Ellen. Evidently, she volunteered at a school. From the writing, it looks like a letter from a young child," says Essie.

"Yes, Jericho School is written in the heading. It should be easy to find out something about a school in this area, even as far back as 1866. Another thing: the card is dated May 11. Didn't Mary Ellen marry Thaddeus in May of 1866?"

"Yes, that's the date carved in the cabinet. Strange. We have a long way to go to solve the mystery. But we have learned two things today—Mary Ellen wrote for a newspaper, and she volunteered at a school called Jericho. That's something. Now, I have to call it a day and start getting ready for Sunday dinner."

Gathering up the photo book, the newspaper articles, and the note cards, Ellen follows Essie down the stairs, wondering if she should start a hope chest. What would she put in it?

Chapter Five
Mary Ellen Davis

Friday, April 6, 1866

Mary Ellen, looking in the parlor mirror at Revival House, ties her bonnet. She does her best to ignore her mother.

"Mary Ellen, you are not going to that school unless Louis drives you. I'm not going to repeat that, young lady."

"Yes, Mother. I understand. Louis has to drive me to Jericho School."

Turning, Mary Ellen looks her mother in the eye.

"Oh, Mary Ellen. Don't sulk. Now, don't you look beautiful in that new blue bonnet."

Remembering her social graces, Mary Ellen says, "And thank you for buying it for me, Mother."

"Now, Mary Ellen. You know I'm not fishing for compliments. Come here and give your mother a kiss."

Mary Ellen obliges before hurrying out the front door to meet Louis. Louis has been at Revival House as long as anyone can remember, and the household would not run smoothly without his presence. Louis runs errands, does handyman jobs, and chauffeurs young ladies.

Louis helps Mary Ellen up into the buggy while asking, "We going to that Jericho school, right?"

"Sure are, Louis. You know the way?"

"Yes, ma'am."

"Well, Louis, let's go see what we shall see."

***

Louis turns the buggy off the Grove Hill Highway onto a long dirt driveway lined with old oak trees. The driveway circles around a decaying two-story home with broken panes in its tall windows and ends at what must be the kitchen: a wooden structure with a chimney and double doors.

"Whoa up there," says Louis to Bonnie, the horse chosen to pull the buggy today.

Mary Ellen notices small faces peering through the bottoms of the windows on the front wall of the kitchen. Their inquisitive faces suggest these children want to know who is visiting their school.

The front door opens, and a man limps out. Mary Ellen would be hard put to describe him. He is an average-looking man of average height and size who has sandy-colored hair that falls into his eyes. The man Mary Ellen assumes is the teacher walks toward the buggy.

"Good morning. May I help you?"

"Good morning to you. I'm Miss Mary Ellen Davis, and I am employed at the *Marshall Times-Standard.* With your permission, I'd like to write a story about your Jericho School."

"Well, welcome Miss Davis. I'm Thomas Brown Mitchell. And you are accompanied by?"

"This is Louis. He's part of our family and never lets me go anywhere alone."

Smiling, Thomas Brown shakes Louis' hand and says, "Well, welcome to you both. Would you like to come in?"

"I would," says Mary Ellen, extending her hand for Thomas Brown to help her from the buggy.

"And you, Louis?" asks Mr. Mitchell.

"I'll wait with the buggy, Mr. Mitchell."

***

Walking into the Jericho School, Mary Ellen's first impression is one of comfortable dignity. Rectangular tables have wooden benches on each long side of the table. Underneath the benches are woven baskets that appear to be assigned to each of the students sitting above them. Mary Ellen sees lunch buckets, some slates, and books spilling out of the baskets. There are five rectangular tables in the room that are placed on top of what appears to be a worn oriental rug.

Blackboards line a long wall without windows. Maps are hung low along the back wall: maps of North America, South America, and Europe hang at just the right height for the smallest child to trace a river with his finger or discover a country he's just studied.

The children are well-disciplined. Even though Mary Ellen can tell they are curious about her, due to their sideways looks in her direction, they continue to work. Mary Ellen counts nineteen children of all ages and gender.

"I'm so impressed with the self-discipline of these children, Mr. Mitchell. May I ask you some questions while they are studying?"

Thomas Brown smiles. "You have about ten minutes until the children finish their lessons, and we move on to science."

Not wanting to waste a minute, Mary Ellen begins. "Why do you call this the Jericho School?"

"My mother taught before she married. Her first school was in the Jericho community, and I knew it would please her, my naming the school Jericho."

"I understood the children had to work in the fields, yet here you are with nineteen children to teach. Was it difficult for you to gather these students?"

"Well, I started with one or two children and the word spread. I was teaching a few hours a day under a tree at the edge of a cotton field. Every week, more and more children came to listen, with their parents' permission, of course. I realized the children were there to stay and got permission to use this kitchen. Better than the cotton field, don't you think?"

Thomas Brown smiled, and Mary Ellen was amazed at how the smile transformed his face. Not so average-looking after all.

"Why do you think the parents excused your students from work in the field?" she asked him. "Because it's April, and it won't be time to pick cotton until August?"

"I'm answering your question with a question. How much do you know about sharecropping?"

"Not much."

"To really explain the system, I need more than ten minutes. Let me just say parents of my students don't want them to be sharecroppers. That's why they are in my class."

"Mr. Mitchell, I know education is the chain breaker. I applaud these parents of yours who want their children educated. Changing the subject, are your students grouped by age or achievement?"

"I have three groups of students in my classroom. First are the young children who are just learning to read and write. Abecedarians they're called. I have an advanced group that is studying world literature and beginning the study of algebra. And the middle group studies American authors and arithmetic.

When I teach science, it's difficult. Today, the entire school is studying photosynthesis, but each of the three levels is doing a different activity related to photosynthesis. Keeps me on my toes. And that's why I have to beg your leave to continue our conversation at another time."

"Of course. I'm sorry for taking you away from your students."

"I assure you, it's not a problem."

"I'd love to come back. May I? And is there a better time for me to visit?"

"Why don't you come back around two o'clock.? Students are working on assignments at that time. Come, say, Tuesday."

"I'd love to come then, but I warn you: I'll have lots of questions."

Thomas Brown smiles. "I think I can field any question you send my way."

After walking Mary Ellen outside to the buggy, Thomas Brown says, "Louis, Miss Davis is coming back next Tuesday. Will I see you then, too?"

"Yes, sir. Where Miss Mary Ellen goes, I go," says Louis.

"Then I look forward to seeing you both on Tuesday."

Turning, Thomas walks up the steps and into the school.

Turning the buggy around, Louis asks, "Did you get enough information to start your story?"

"Not today, Louis. But I hope I will on Tuesday. I can tell you, Louis, I'm fascinated."

Visit Ellen's Notebook at the end of the book to see a picture of the kitchen behind the Garvey Plantation House.

Chapter Six
Mary Ellen Davis

Saturday, April 7, 1866

"Mary Ellen, the dessert fork lies at the top of the plate. You'll never find a husband if you don't know your forks."

"Yes, Mother." Frowning, Mary Ellen removes the fork in question from the side to the top of the plate and places it horizontally. "Why do we need to go to so much trouble for this Thaddeus Baird? So, what if he's the son of Dad's college roommate?"

"Young lady, we always go to trouble for guests at Revival House. And he might be a prospect."

"A prospect?" Mary Ellen is pretty sure she knows what her mother means.

"For marriage, girl. I swear, I just don't understand you, Mary Ellen." Standing back to observe the table, Mrs. Davis nods. "When we get the fresh bouquet in the middle of the table, everything will be perfect. Now, why don't you go upstairs and powder your nose?"

"Yes, Mother," Mary Ellen repeats. There's no use arguing with her mother all the time. Acknowledging it is better to have peace in the family, Mary Ellen quietly goes up to her room.

***

Sitting at her dressing table, Mary Ellen lightly dusts her face with powder to make it look pale, then adds a small dot of rouge to the center of her lips and another dot below the outer corner of the eye. These actions make up the sum total of Ellen's cosmetics. After all, no respectable woman wears face paints. An intervention was conducted for Gladys Johnson at the Methodist ladies' Sunday School class when she painted her lips bright red before coming to church.

Seeing the notes she took at the Jericho School on the vanity, Mary Ellen picks them up and starts to read. Soon she is writing down questions to ask at her next visit. Mary Ellen is so engrossed in her questions she doesn't hear the door to her room open.

"Doodle, you better get downstairs right away. Our illustrious dinner guest—Adam rolls his eyes—has arrived, and Mother is beginning to twitch because you're not down."

"Well, blazes. I'm coming," says Mary Ellen.

"You better not let Mother hear you swearing," says Adam.

"I won't. Now come on. Let's go meet this illustrious guest." Mary Ellen smiles at Adam and puts her arm through his.

***

As Ellen walks into the dining room, Mary Ellen's mother indicates with a nod of her head that Mary Ellen is to sit by Thaddeus Baird. Resigning herself to a boring meal where she's stuck eating and not working on her story, Ellen stands next to Thaddeus while noting he's extremely handsome, if you like the dark and brooding kind.

"Thaddeus, this is my daughter, Mary Ellen. She's been looking forward to meeting you, as have we all," says Mary Ellen's mother. Mary Ellen notices Adam's smirk across the table but chooses to ignore it.

"Delighted to meet you, Miss Davis," says Thaddeus.

"Delighted to meet you as well, Mr. Baird," says Mary Ellen.

"Please, I hope all of you will call me Thaddeus."

"We'll be pleased to do so, Thaddeus," says Mary Ellen's father as he walks into the dining room. "Please be seated. All of you. Now, Thaddeus, are you all settled over at Howard?"

"Yes, the college has been kind enough to provide housing for me on campus—a dorm room. I eat all my meals in the college cafeteria. I'm on my own during the weekend."

"And, your father didn't say, what are you studying?"

"American literature. I hope to be able to teach at the University of Alabama one day."

"I'm sure you'll do just that," says Mary Ellen's father. "Did you know our Mary Ellen is a writer?"

Turning to look at Mary Ellen, Thaddeus says, "Well, how wonderful. What do you write?"

When Thaddeus looks at her, Mary Ellen gets a strange, warm feeling. This man is handsome. "I write for the *Marshall Times-Standard.* I'm currently working on a story about one of our soldiers who has opened a school for sharecroppers' children."

"That sounds interesting. Have you seen the school?"

"I've only been once but am going back next week to interview the teacher, Mr. Mitchell."

"I over-scheduled next week but would love to visit the school with you one day, since I hope to be a teacher."

"I'll ask Mr. Mitchell; I'm sure he'll approve of your visit."

"Well done, Mary Ellen. Now Thaddeus, tell me about your father, that rascal of a roommate of mine," says Mary Ellen's father.

Chapter Seven
Mary Ellen Davis

Tuesday, April 10. 1866

Looking around the Jericho schoolroom, Mary Ellen notices all the touches Thomas Brown has added to the old kitchen that's now become a schoolroom. She noticed the oriental rug and baskets before, but now she sees low shelves under the two windows filled with all sorts of books, tumbled in all directions. It's an appealing sight—makes you want to choose a book from the chaos and settle down to read.

Two tufted armchairs, just right for curling up and reading, are placed at the front of the room and to the right of the teacher's desk. Plants in an assortment of mostly chipped cups and tin cans that once held baking powder and coffee line the window sill; Mary Ellen assumes the plants tie in with the lesson on photosynthesis.

After Thomas Brown gives assignments to each of the three groups of learners, he walks to where Mary Ellen is standing at the front of the room and motions for her to sit in one of the two tufted chairs. Sitting down, Thomas Brown asks, "And now, Miss Davis, during your last visit, you asked about sharecropping. What would you like to know?"

"How does it work? How do sharecroppers earn a living? I have a general idea but want to be accurate for my article," says Mary Ellen.

"We'll start with sharecroppers earning wages. The plantation owners own the land and provide the sharecropper land, seed, fertilizer, a mule, and a plow. If a sharecropper owns his own mule and plow, he will make more money from the harvest."

"Is it cotton they are planting?"

"Oh, yes. The sharecroppers plow, chop, hoe, and pick the cotton. Half of the bales go to the plantation owner, and the sharecroppers don't earn any money until the harvest is gathered."

"So, how do they live if they have to wait for the harvest to get money?"

"They get what they need from the plantation commissary. Since they don't have money, they charge. Much of their annual wages go to pay off the commissary debt."

"It seems to me that the sharecroppers are stuck in a vicious cycle with no way out. How do they improve their lives?"

"They may not be able to, but their children can. That's why they are here, and it's why I do what I do. Do you know, just a couple of years ago I could have been arrested for teaching colored children?"

"No."

"Yes. When the parents of these children were slaves, they were forbidden to learn to read and write, and I would have been arrested for teaching them."

Ellen sits quietly to absorb what she's just heard, then she reacts, "That's absurd. I've never heard of anything so ridiculous. Why?"

Mary Ellen glances at the students, no longer bent over their slates but looking at her, and realizes she is upsetting them. She silently vows to be quieter.

Thomas Brown continues in a lower voice, "A literate slave population would present a threat to the plantation owners. At least, that's what the owners thought. They wanted their slaves to be dependent."

"Well, Mr. Mitchell, what you're doing here is one of the most admirable things I've ever encountered. Ever in my life."

"Well, Miss Davis, why don't you join me?"

"Me?" Reaching her hand up to her throat, Mary Ellen swallows. "Me?" she says again.

"Yes, you—Miss Mary Ellen Davis."

"But what could I do?"

"It's hard for me to teach three groups of students. I feel like I'm juggling, trying to keep everything up in the air and running smoothly. If you supervised a group after I've given them directions, it would be a huge help. Especially if you came on Friday. I concentrate on the advanced students on Friday and often test them. It would be beneficial to everyone if you were here to work with the other two groups."

"It's a lot to think about, and I do have my job at the *Times-Standard*."

"Just think about it. You can let me know when you've reached a decision."

"I will think about it, Mr. Mitchell. Oh, I forgot. The son of my father's college roommate is in Marion for the summer. When he came to dinner, we discussed the work you're doing, and he'd like to visit. Mr. Baird is his name. He wants to be a university teacher and is studying with Professor Goodhue this summer."

"Of course, he's welcome. Especially if you come with him."

My goodness! Is Mr. Mitchell flirting with me?

"Of course, I'll accompany Mr. Baird. Would this time next Tuesday work?"

"That's fine. The students are adaptable and would probably enjoy another visitor."

"I have to get in touch with Mr. Baird. If Tuesday is convenient for him, Louis will bring you confirmation."

"I'm interested in Louis. Can he read and write?"

"Absolutely. Louis would be incensed if he heard your question."

"Maybe he can read to the younger children, while you work with the middle group. That's if you agree to work with me."

"I am not sure. We're moving rather quickly, don't you think?"

Thomas Brown smiles, "Not when it comes to educating these children."

"If Mr. Baird is available next Tuesday, I'll give you my answer then. I probably need to discuss this with my parents."

"Yes, it's wise to include your parents in this decision. Now, if you're ready, I'll have Benjamin walk you to your buggy. Benjamin, please come help Miss Davis."

Mary Ellen watches as a boy of maybe ten years old puts down his slate and walks to where they are standing.

"Benjamin, this is Miss Davis and, if we're lucky, she will be here every Friday."

Mary Ellen crouches to be at eye level with Benjamin. "Hello, Benjamin, so very nice to meet you."

Benjamin smiles the widest smile, revealing one missing front tooth, and Mary Ellen's heart melts. Standing up, she extends her hand to Benjamin for a handshake. "Thank you so much for walking me to my buggy, Benjamin," she says.

Benjamin bows and says, "My pleasure." He looks to Thomas Brown for approval, seeming relieved when his teacher smiles at him.

Thomas Brown mouths the words, "I'm trying."

Mary Ellen smiles and nods.

As they walk out the door to the school, Mary Ellen asks, "Benjamin, what is your favorite subject?"

"Literature. I love the stories! I want to write. I am going to grow up and write novels, and everyone will read them and carry on over them."

"That is a noble ambition. Did you know I'm a writer?"

Benjamin stops and looks up at Mary Ellen. "No, ma'am."

"Yes, but I write newspaper stories. For the *Times-Standard*. I'm writing a story about Jericho School right now. I'll make sure you get a copy of the article, along with Mr. Mitchell, of course."

"Thank you, ma'am. I will be especially excited to read it."

At the buggy, Ellen introduces Louis to the enthusiastic student. Benjamin extends his hand to Louis, "My pleasure."

Hiding a smile, Louis replies, "The pleasure is mine."

"I hope to see you next Tuesday, Benjamin," says Mary Ellen, getting in the buggy.

"I sure hope so, Miss Davis," says Benjamin.

As they drive away, Louis looks back toward the school. Benjamin has not moved. His eyes follow the buggy as it drives away.

Clearing his throat, Louis says, "I think you have an admirer."

"Well," says Mary Ellen, "Benjamin has one, too."

Chapter Eight
Mary Ellen Davis

Sunday, April 15, 1866

Mary Ellen fidgets on the church pew in the Methodist Episcopal Church South, receiving a stern look from her mother. She is looking forward to Sunday dinner with Sara's fried chicken. Ah, the pastor is asking the congregation to stand for the first three verses of "Just As I Am," a sure sign the service is coming to an end.

Standing, the congregation sings:

> *But that Thy blood was shed for me,*
> *And that Thou bidst me come to Thee,*
> *O Lamb of God, I come, I come.*

Looking around, Mary Ellen spots Thaddeus Baird standing alone across the aisle. He is singing with a booming voice; Mary Ellen can understand every word.

Just as I am, and waiting not
To rid my soul of one dark blot...

Thaddeus looks up from his hymnal and notices Mary Ellen. He stops singing, smiles, and bows his head, acknowledging her. Mary Ellen is flustered; she sings the wrong verse, blushes, and quickly corrects her mistake.

As the third verse fades away, the pastor thanks the congregation for attending, reminds them of the Wednesday night service, and says, "Go forth, and be children of God."

Thaddeus makes his way to the Davis family, bowing to Mr. Davis when he arrives at their pew.

"Thaddeus, what a pleasant surprise. You can walk home with us."

"Yes, I thought since I'm having dinner with you, I might as well join you for the service. I have no church in Marion yet." Bowing again, he turns to the group. "And good morning to you, Mrs. Davis, Mr. Adam, and Miss Davis."

"We are so pleased to see you, Thaddeus, and look forward to your dining with us. Come, let's walk home," her mother motions to them. "Sara is waiting with her excellent fried chicken."

Bowing again, Thaddeus says, "I'll follow your lead, Mrs. Davis." He follows Mrs. Davis down the church aisle, but once outside, he drops back.

Am I imagining it? Is Thaddeus deliberately trying to walk beside me?

"Miss Davis, I am looking forward to hearing about your Jericho School. And have you gotten Mr. Mitchell's approval for me to visit?"

Mary Ellen forgets all about being nervous around Thaddeus. "Oh, yes. If it fits your calendar, we both are to visit the school this coming Tuesday at two o'clock. Does that fit your schedule?"

"Yes, I…"

"Wonderful. I can't wait until you see how Mr. Mitchell has converted the plantation kitchen into a schoolhouse. It is so warm and inviting. Books scattered everywhere to pick up and read. Armchairs to fold yourself into in order to read. And wait until you see how Mr. Mitchell has organized his classes. Oh, you will be so impressed." Stopping to catch her breath, Mary Ellen looks up to see an amused expression on Thaddeus' face.

"Well, how I do go on," says Mary Ellen. Straightening her shoulders, she puts a serious expression on her face.

Thaddeus laughs. "Please, Miss Davis, do not get so serious. I love your enthusiasm for the school and am sure I'll feel the same."

Smiling, Mary Ellen replies, "Well, I hope so."

Thaddeus laughs again, getting Mr. Davis' attention, who walks back to join the two.

"What's this?"

"Miss Davis was painting a picture of the Jericho School for me. With your permission, I plan to meet Miss Davis at the school on Tuesday. I'm looking forward to talking with Mr. Mitchell and seeing his school."

"Well, I say, Mary Ellen is captivated. I'm sure you will enjoy your visit. Now, come in our home. We look forward to hearing the news from Marion."

***

Once again, Mrs. Davis has placed Mary Ellen beside Thaddeus at the dining room table. Looking at Thaddeus as he talks, Mary Ellen is struck by his good looks—his dark hair and mustache and just a tint of olive to his skin. *There's no one this handsome in Marshall, and, so far, I like him.* She considers the thought, then shakes it loose to return to the dinner conversation.

Midst the passing of Sara's fried chicken and vegetables, dinner conversation turns to a meeting to be held in Montgomery tomorrow morning. "Leave it to the ladies," says Mr. Davis. "They'll bring home our Confederate dead."

"What do you mean, Father?" asks Mary Ellen.

"I am talking about the Confederate soldiers still lying on battlefields in Alabama. The Federal Government has already sent scouts to gather Union soldiers and take them

49

home for burial in the United States National Cemetery. Currently, there are no plans for Confederate soldiers as most Alabamians just don't have the money needed to locate their dead and bring them home."

"And the ladies—what do they have to do with it?" asks Mrs. Davis.

"A group of ladies are meeting at ten in the morning at the Court Street Methodist Episcopal Church in Montgomery for the purpose of organizing a committee to raise funds to bring home the Confederate dead."

"How do you know this, Mr. Davis?" asks Mrs. Davis.

"I know because Margaret Bell of our town of Marshall will be attending. She is going to propose the committee calls itself The Ladies Society for the Burial of Deceased Alabama Soldiers."

"This society is certainly an important one. Mary Ellen, you may want to interview Miss Bell for the paper," says Mrs. Davis.

"I agree, Mother," says Mary Ellen. This brings a shocked look to Adam's face. Mary Ellen never agrees with her mother. "But don't forget, I'm working on the Jericho School story, too."

During the dinner conversation, Molly, the family Cocker Spaniel, makes her way under the dining table, stepping over feet as she goes. Molly stops to lick Thaddeus' ankle, and Mary Ellen is shocked to see Thaddeus give

Molly a swift kick in the stomach. Molly yelps, and Mrs. Davis lifts the tablecloth.

"Molly, what are you doing under there? I know Sara fed you just an hour ago. Oh, never mind. Come here, and I'll give you a bite of chicken," says Mrs. Davis.

Mary Ellen doesn't look at Thaddeus Baird. She's shocked at his treatment of Molly. Distracted by Sara's passing of dessert, Mary Ellen soon forgets Molly as talk swirls of events on the Howard campus. Waiting until everyone has finished their dessert and risen from the table, Thaddeus thanks Mrs. Davis for the hospitality and expresses his regret that he has to return to campus.

"I will look forward to seeing you on Tuesday, Miss Davis. I certainly look forward to it." Mary Ellen is flustered by his intense stare.

"What do you say, Mary Ellen?" asks Mrs. Davis.

"I look forward to Tuesday as well." *What an idiot! I sound like an idiot.*

Chapter Nine
Ellen Jones

Sunday, March 18, 1962

Sunday dinner at Essie's is a raucous affair—everyone talking at the same time around the long dining room table while plates of fried pork chops and yams are passed. Essie is bustling around, bringing in more vegetable dishes from the outdoor kitchen. Julio, David's son, and his girlfriend, Carol, are talking with Amanda about Marion, the small town where Carol lives and where Julio attends Marion Military Institute. Zia and David are talking with Will and Amanda; David is telling about his work producing sugar.

"I have always worked with sugar cane before it goes to a refinery. I enjoy harvesting it, extracting the juice from the cane, and boiling it until the syrup thickens and crystallizes. Then you have to make raw sugar…"

"David, you are boring them to death," says Zia, squeezing his hand.

"No, he's not," says Will. "And I will have questions for you about this sugar-making process as we think about enlarging our own production. But right now I have some questions about Cuba. We know Zia was accidentally caught up in a conspiracy to kill Castro." Turning his head to look at Zia, Will asks, "Right?"

"You are correct," says Zia. "The militia in Cuba terrified me. They spit on us and cursed us. One day I was home alone and, looking out the window, I saw a formation of militia marching down our street in Miramar. I panicked. I ran across the street to a restaurant; I knew the owner and felt I would be safer there. Little did I know, the owner along with other Cubans and even a few CIA men were in the process of plotting the assignation of Castro at that very moment. I was swept up along with the conspirators and taken to La Cabaña, a terrible fortress where prisoners were lined up on a firing line and killed as a daily occurrence."

"Yet you are here," says Amanda. "And we are thankful for it. Thankful every day you are out of Castro's world."

"Have you heard any of the rumors about attempts on Castro's life?" asks Will.

"But, of course," answers David. "Under the Eisenhower administration, mob members from the FBI's Most Wanted List tried to give Castro a poison pill. That's the rumor. Don't know how they were to manage that, but it failed."

"And don't forget," says Zia. "Castro's lover, Marita Lorenz, was to drop a poisonous pill into Castro's drink, but she made a mistake. Marita put the pill in a face cream jar for safe keeping, and the face cream turned the pill to mush."

"Most bizarre of all—it's rumored that a couple of years ago the CIA planned to spoil a speech given by Castro by spraying the studio with a hallucination-induced spray. All rumors, but 'where there's smoke, there's fire,'" says David.

"Castro seems to be like the proverbial cat with nine lives," says Will.

"Unfortunately," says David, remembering that Castro had cost him his daughter and his country.

Essie puts down a bowl of collard greens and a plate of cornbread. "Now, eat up everybody. There's sour cream pound cake for dessert."

Reaching for the hot cornbread, David says, "You spoil us, Essie."

***

"You do spoil us, Essie." She and Essie are alone in the parlor. Essie has the newspaper articles from Mary Ellen's trunk in her lap. Before they begin going through the stack of articles, Ellen turns to her aunt and asks, "Did you ever see such love as Zia's and David's? I sure hope I find that kind of love. How about you, Essie? Did you and Uncle James have that kind of marriage?"

"I am afraid not, and I take the blame for it."

"Why? What happened, Aunt Essie?"

"It's a sad ol' tale—one we in the family stay away from. You sure you want to hear it?"

"If it involves you, I want to hear about it."

"I was always in love with someone else. A boy I grew up with. When he died of scarlet fever at age sixteen, I died a little with him. I certainly didn't want to marry anyone else, but my parents insisted. There was a stigma attached to girls who were sixteen and not married. So, I let my parents talk me into marrying James."

"How could you, Aunt Essie? You didn't love him."

"No. Never did."

"Does the wedding dress that wasn't white figure into this?"

"Yes, that was my one rebellion. I refused to wear a white dress. It was shocking since such a dress indicated an impure bride. I was pure, but rebellious."

"Aunt Essie, you were forced into a marriage you didn't want. How can you take the blame for a failed marriage?"

"Because I didn't try. James cheated on me and, looking back, I don't blame him."

"That's so sad, Aunt Essie."

"Maybe. But it was scandalous as well, because James ran away to Texas with the church secretary. I hear they are still living in Texas. They've had children, and, as far as I know, a good marriage."

"Weren't you horrified? He cheated on you."

"One thing I am—honest with myself. My fault for being talked into a marriage I didn't want."

"It *is* a sad tale, Essie."

"Now, don't you dare feel sorry for me. I have the best family in the world, and there is a man in Selma I'm learning to care about. Not a word, Ellen Jones. The man in Selma is my secret. And now yours."

"Oh, I'm so happy for you, Essie. I bet this man is the explanation for the new Essie look. Is this man good looking?"

"Drop-dead gorgeous." says Essie, laughing. "Now, we need to get to these articles from the trunk. But about my friend, 'And the Lord make you to increase and abound in love one toward another... 1 Thessalonians 3:1.' Enough now! Let's get back to Mary Ellen and this mystery of ours."

Ellen picks up a small leather book that was hidden among all the articles and cards. Opening to the front page, she sees the book is a journal belonging to Mary Ellen. Midway through the journal, Ellen finds a heart that fills most of the page. *Mary Ellen and Thaddeus* is written inside the heart. On the next journal page, *Mrs. Thaddeus Baird* is written over and over. Showing the book to Essie, Ellen says, "Here's proof our Mary Ellen was infatuated with Thaddeus Baird."

"Yes, but what about Thomas Brown Mitchell?"

"Okay, Aunt Essie, you take the note cards, and I'll take the newspaper articles. Let's see if we can find Thomas Brown." Putting the journal aside, Ellen sorts through the cards and newspaper articles brought down from the attic, dividing them into stacks. Ellen hands the cards to Essie and starts reading from the top article.

The first two articles are about Marshall College, but the third is just what Ellen is looking for—an article written for the *Marshall Times-Standard* about the Jericho School. The article is written by Mary Ellen Davis.

Garvey Plantation Alive Again with Student Learning

Marshall, Ala., April 20 — Thomas Brown Mitchell, a war veteran, is teaching sharecroppers' children in the kitchen behind the old Garvey Plantation mansion. What started as lessons under a tree at the edge of a cotton field has become a classroom filled with books for the reading, comfortable chairs in which to read, and a teacher who says he cares deeply about furthering the education of these young children.

Mitchell stated, "I believe these children can rise above. They are not destined to work in the fields. They are only limited by their drive and their imagination."

Prior to the war, Mitchell graduated with honors from the University of Alabama. He entered the war only seven months prior to its end. His knee was damaged by a musket ball at Fort Blakeley, as Union troops sought to flush out the last of the confederate soldiers along the Alabama coast. Oddly, the battle of Fort Blakely was fought the same day Lee surrendered at Appomattox.

Mitchell chose the Garvey Plantation because it belongs to a relative of his mother's. Although the plantation house is in ruins, Mitchell knew the kitchen, which is separated from the house, could be made into a schoolroom. He has always loved the old house and carries memories of dancing at family parties, picking pecans from the numerous pecan trees on the place, and shivering from the old stories of ghosts rising from hidden tunnels.

Thomas Brown Mitchell looks ahead to the day his students graduate from colleges and universities across the South.

Mary Ellen Davis

"Well, that tells us something about Thomas Brown. He sounds just like someone I'd want Mary Ellen to marry," says Ellen.

Essie fans out the note cards. "Most of these cards are written from students to Mary Ellen. Some thank her for working with them on Fridays. Some thank her for inspiring them to write. It seems she definitely volunteered with Thomas Brown at the Jericho School."

"But why did she marry him? She seems to be in love with Thaddeus Baird," ask Ellen.

"A mystery for sure. And Jericho School is a part of the mystery," says Essie. "I do think we are making progress, and I have another idea. There is someone still living near here who worked at the Revival House when Mary Ellen was growing up. Lottie is her name. I think she'll be delighted with a visit from us. We will solve this, Ellen. One step at a time."

Chapter Ten
Mary Ellen Davis

Tuesday, April 17, 1866

When Louis pulls up to Jericho School, Mary Ellen notices a strange buggy, indicating Thaddeus must already be in the schoolhouse. Louis helps Mary Ellen down from the buggy. "Louis, Mr. Mitchell would like you to come inside. Would you like that?"

"No ma'am."

Surprised, Mary Ellen asks, "Are you sure?"

"Yes, ma'am. I'll come in sometime when Mr. Baird ain't here."

Mary Ellen knows Louis won't answer her question but asks anyway. "Don't you like Mr. Baird?"

"I don't know him, Miss Mary Ellen." Louis has no expression on his face.

"Well, have it your way, Louis. I'll make your regrets to Mr. Mitchell."

"Yes, ma'am."

Walking into the schoolroom, Mary Ellen notices the students are working on their slates, and the two men are talking.

Interrupting, Mary Ellen says, "I see you two have met."

Thomas Brown's face lights up. "Miss Davis, delighted to see you. I was just explaining my levels of instruction to Mr. Baird."

Thaddeus smiles at Mary Ellen. "I'm delighted to see you as well."

When Thaddeus talks to Mary Ellen, his voice oozes. Mary Ellen is not sure what it oozes, but ooze it does. That warm feeling is back. Mary Ellen prays she is not blushing.

Nodding her head, she says, "It good to see the two of you. And I still have questions for Mr. Mitchell. I'm sure you do, too, Mr. Baird."

"Yes, but I will defer to you, Miss Davis."

"Just this month, despite President Andrew Johnson, Congress passed the Civil Rights Bill of 1866, granting the rights of citizenship to colored people. This is a step in the right direction, but we still have so far to go. For example, I can attend Marshall College, but these students of yours cannot. They need to move from your classroom to advanced programs. How do they do that?" asks Mary Ellen.

"They will come—colleges for the colored—and I want my students to be ready. There is a rumor going around about such a college opening next year in Atlanta. What a fine thing."

"Yes, I heard talk of that very thing on campus last week. And I agree with you. Kudos to the organizers making a colored college happen. And I have a question about your curriculum. What are your advanced students studying?" asks Thaddeus.

"World literature and algebra."

"And your middle group?"

"American literature and arithmetic"

"I am studying American literature at Howard. What is your curriculum?"

"I follow the curriculum for the local male academy. My students and I look at the culture and the literature of America from the Colonial Period through the Early National period of the United States."

"I studied the same but also studied works from the beginnings of the Romantic Period. What works have your students studied so far?"

"We started with Mark Twain, then studied Walt Whitman, and we are currently studying the poetry of Phillis Wheatley. These students are electrified by the thought of one of their own being published—and her a slave at that."

"That's brilliant. I need to include Wheatley's poetry in my own readings."

While the two men are discussing curriculum, Mary Ellen walks over to the students. Not wanting to interrupt, she quietly paces through the rows of children until Benjamin gets her attention. He is sitting at the end of the row and appears to be working arithmetic problems on his slate. Mary Ellen sees that he has the answer to the first problem correct: 1 is 5% of 20.

Mary Ellen notices the little girl sitting next to Benjamin. She has two plaits meant to hang down her back but one is currently in her mouth: she is chewing on the end of the plait. Chewing in frustration, it seems.

Thomas whispers, "That's Ruth. She can't do math; but, boy, can she write. We're great friends."

Realizing they are talking about her, Ruth looks up to meet Mary Ellen's eyes. Mary Ellen's first thought—*she's beautiful*. Her eyes seem to fill her face and are a deep shade of green. After taking Mary Ellen in, Ruth smiles and whispers, "I dislike arithmetic."

Mary Ellen smiles and whispers back, "It is fine to dislike it, but we have to have it, you know. Even famous writers need arithmetic."

Fascinated, Ruth asks, "Why?"

"When you are a famous author, you will need to know how to handle all the money you'll make from writing novels. Or is it something else you'd like to write?"

"Oh, I want to write the best novel ever."

Mary Ellen smiles a broad smile that covers the lower part of her face. "Then you will. And I will be one of the first to read it."

Mary Ellen puts her index finger to her lips, not wanting to disturb any of the students further. Walking back toward the two men, Mary Ellen notices they are saying their goodbyes and says, "I hope you enjoyed your visit and are as impressed as I am." Her remark is aimed at Thaddeus.

"I certainly am impressed. Now, may I walk you to your carriage?"

"Thank you, but I need a moment with Mr. Mitchell."

"Then I'll say goodbye until we meet again." Thaddeus smiles at Mary Ellen, bows, and leaves.

Watching Thaddeus cross the room, Mary Ellen notices again what a fine man he is.

Interrupting her thoughts, Thomas Brown says, "Yes, Miss Davis?"

Mary Ellen is embarrassed that she's been caught admiring the backside of the handsome Mr. Baird.

"I discussed your proposal about teaching on Fridays, and my parents approve as long as Louis is with me."

"How excellent! I'm so thankful. Will you be able to start this Friday?"

"Yes. Louis and I will see you Friday."

"Wonderful. **Benjamin** is taking a test, or I would have him walk you to your buggy. He is rather in awe of you."

"And I him." Mary Ellen smiles in **Benjamin**'s direction. "But I can see myself out. Thank you for having us, and I will be here Friday."

"I will forever be in your debt." Thomas Brown bows to Mary Ellen who turns and walks by the rows of students and out of the school that will be her Friday home. It is a pleasant thought. *Her Friday home.*

Chapter Eleven
Ellen Jones

Monday, March 19, 1962

Dropping a half-eaten piece of sugar cinnamon toast on her breakfast plate, Ellen answers Amanda, "I'm exploring a feature story on our first lady for my next *Miami News Now* story. I don't want to cover what she wears or how her hair is styled. I want to dig inside the real Jackie. What do you think?"

"I am surprised you have waited to do this story. Our first lady of Camelot is interesting, indeed. What have you learned from your research that I wouldn't know?"

"Jackie's first grade teachers described her as clever, artistic, and a troublemaker—a student who was often sent to the headmistress. That's not how we imagine her, is it?"

"Of course not. Beautiful, poised Jackie Kennedy an unruly student? I think it makes me like her a little more."

"Me, too," says Ellen. "She's human."

"You know, I want to read your story when you finish."

"I'll make sure you get a copy. Now—once again—I've got to leave you and go to Essie's. I believe we are going to visit a lady named Lottie. Want help with the dishes before I go?"

"No. Shoo. See you for dinner?"

Grabbing her coat, Ellen smiles at Amanda, "Of course."

***

Lottie lives in Dry Valley. To get to Dry Valley, turn off Highway 13 going south out of Marshall onto Dry Valley Road. It's all the name implies. Off a lonely, one-lane road. Without rain, it's so dusty the bushes on each side of the road wear shrouds of light-brown powder. Ellen's throat tickles just looking at it.

Dogtrot houses, with their large, open halls running through the middle of the house, are spaced evenly apart on the road. Most have a field for planting near them. Lottie's home, fifth on the right after you turn on Dry Valley Road, is constructed of wide, unpainted planks with a front porch and a smoking stone fireplace, which must be the source of the mild, sweet smell in the air.

A small elderly lady, hair pulled back tight against her scalp, stops rocking in her chair as Ellen and Aunt Essie walk up toward the house. At the same time, dogs, who were curled up under Lottie's clapboard house, come out en masse, barking at the top of their lungs.

"Hush up now, hounds. This is just Miss Essie from town. Who's that beauty with you, Miss Essie?"

"This is my niece, Ellen. Will's daughter. Ellen is helping me solve a mystery. We hope you can help, too."

"Well, come on up on this porch and sit down," Lottie says, nodding toward the two ladder-back chairs on the porch. "It's a drive out here to the valley. Would you like some of my almond tea served over ice cubes?"

Essie answers for both of them. "We'd love it. I remember your almond tea—the best around." Once they are settled on the porch, Essie starts. "Lottie, we need some information about the Davis family. Actually, we need to know something about Mary Ellen. I know you worked for Mason and Olivia for years. We want to know about the time Mary Ellen worked at the Jericho School. In 1866."

"I remember Miss Mary Ellen like it was yesterday. I was a child myself at the time, and I'd never seen a girl like Miss Mary Ellen. Working at the newspaper and teaching at that school for sharecropper children. I always admired her."

"We'd love to hear what you remember about that time, especially if it involves Mary Ellen," says Essie.

"Oh, I have my memories all right. The balls, the Sunday dinners, the Thanksgiving feasts. Special as all get out."

"The Sunday dinners. Do you remember a man about my age coming to Sunday dinner? Thaddeus Baird was his name," says Ellen.

"I do. I remember him. Didn't care for him. Sara and Louis didn't either."

"Why?" ask Essie and Ellen at the same time. This is the first thing they have heard about Thaddeus the person.

"Oh, he was handsome all right, and Mary Ellen was smitten with him, but he had a mean streak in him. Louis told me that Baird asked him if he was Mr. Davis' nigger. You know Mr. Davis would not allow that word in his presence. Sara saw him kick the dog under the dining room table, and he bumped into me in the hall, almost pushing me down without as much as an 'I'm sorry.'"

"Oh, Essie. Surely our Mary Ellen didn't love this kind of man," says Ellen.

"It adds more to the mystery, for sure," says Essie.

"The balls, Lottie. What do you remember about the balls? Sounds so romantic," says Ellen.

"That ballroom was something special with the big windows, white columns, and fancy light fixtures hanging from the ceiling. I remember one special ball where they had a fortune teller. Always scared of 'em myself, but the townsfolk seemed to love hearing their fortunes."

"Mary Ellen was there?" asks Ellen.

"Lawd, yes. And she sure was beautiful in a blue dress with a full skirt. It was one of those off-the-shoulder dresses. I can see her in my mind."

"Did you ever hear that she married Thaddeus Baird?"

"Never. I woulda remembered that. She married Mr. Mitchell, that schoolteacher, didn't she?"

"Yes, she did, Lottie. We are just curious about Mr. Baird," says Essie. Standing up, Essie hands Lottie her tea glass. "We have to get back home, Lottie. Thank you for the tea and for talking to us. If you ever need anything you let me know, hear."

"I'm fine, Miss Essie. I thank you for visiting and bringing this beautiful girl with you. Nice to meet you, Miss Ellen."

Ellen smiles at Lottie. "Nice to meet you, too, Miss Lottie."

Walking down the path to the car, Ellen asks, "And just how old is Lottie?"

Essie scrunches up her brow, thinking before answering. "She is probably a hundred years old by now. She'd have to be."

"Gosh, I didn't know people got that old. And she has a good memory."

"Well, Ellen," says Essie, "Gives us something to look forward to. We might live to be a hundred, too."

Chapter Twelve
Mary Ellen Davis

Saturday, April 21, 1866

Mary Ellen is in the kitchen with Sara on the afternoon of one of the famous Davis ballroom affairs.

"Miss Mary Ellen, your mother says you have to eat something before the party. What would you like, leftover chicken or ham? I can put some pickles on the plate and a small piece of apple pie."

"I'll take a little of everything. You don't have to convince me to eat. Oh, Sara, I'm so excited about tonight."

"I can see that. And I hear that Mr. Baird has been invited."

"Yes, he has. Oh, Sara. Isn't he handsome?"

"Well, I can't answer that, Miss Mary Ellen, but I think you are smitten. This is the first time you've mentioned a man, instead of one of those stories you are always writing."

Taking a bite of ham from the plate in front of her, Mary Ellen chews and thinks. *Nothing has ever been more important than journalism. Is Sara right?*

"Have you finished that story about Jericho School?"

"No, but I will soon. Did you know I'm going to work at the school on Fridays?"

"No. How did that come about?"

"Mr. Mitchell needs help, because he has three groups of students, and it is very hard to give each student individual attention. I am going to work with the students after they have received the lesson from Mr. Mitchell."

"That is a good deed you are doing. I'm proud of you."

"Thank you, Sara. But let's talk about the dance. Mother is bringing in a fortune teller to tell fortunes with cards. Don't you think that is scandalous?"

"No ma'am. I hear everyone is doing it at parties. It's just for fun, you know."

"I can't wait to hear my fortune. Not a real one, you know. I don't want to know the future."

"You are a rare one, Miss Mary Ellen. Come let me see how you look before going in the ballroom."

"I will, Sara. See you after I'm beautiful."

"You are always beautiful," Sara says quietly under her breath as Mary Ellen proceeds out the door and heads up the stairs to get ready for the ball.

***

Mary Ellen stands in the receiving line, greeting each guest, for an hour. Guests are dancing to the orchestra stationed at the far end of the ballroom, but it is the food Mary Ellen is interested in. She's ready to get a plate full and sneak away to eat. Turning to the tables lining the wall closest to the door, Mary Ellen gets a silver-rimmed china plate and chooses ham, cold fowl, and crayfish in jelly.

Mary Ellen senses him before she sees him. She turns. Thaddeus, plate in hand, bows. "Would you do me the honor of sitting with me while we eat?"

Before she can stop herself, Mary Ellen says, "I'd love to." Blushing, she realizes she has been perhaps a little too eager. To his credit, Thaddeus does not laugh, but he escorts her to one of the small tables lining the left wall.

Thaddeus pulls out the brocade chair, waits for Mary Ellen to seat herself, and slides the chair toward the table. As he is seating himself, he asks, "Have you had your fortune told?"

"Not yet. But I can't wait. I'm sure she'll tell me I'll meet a tall, dark, handsome man." Mary Ellen blushes, looking at the man who fits such a description sitting across from her.

***

When Mary Ellen has obligated most of the men on her dance card, she goes to see the fortune teller, who is seated outside the ballroom in an alcove. Mary Ellen is surprised to see a polished woman in a white silk blouse who has her blonde hair up in a sophisticated hairdo.

"Sit down, please, Miss Davis," says the fortune teller.

Shocked that the fortune teller knows her name, Mary Ellen obliges. Mary Ellen notices her long nails, polished the lightest shade of pink, as the fortune teller places her right hand on a deck of cards and fans them into a semicircle.

"Now, Miss Davis, pick three cards from the deck, and I will read your fortune."

Mary Ellen runs her fingers over several of the cards before choosing one.

"Please place the card face up on the table."

Mary Ellen turns the card over.

"Ah, the King of Hearts. A fair-haired man. A man with a good nature who is affectionate and caring. Now, the second card, please."

Once again, Mary Ellen takes her time and turns over the Ten of Hearts.

"Wonderful. This is a good-luck card. You will have good fortune after great difficulty."

Feeling good about the cards she has turned over, Mary Ellen turns over the third card. The King of Spades.

The fortune teller seems to hesitate, then says, "The dark man. I'm afraid, my dear, he's an enemy who is to be feared."

A shiver goes up Mary Ellen's spine. *A ghost walked over your grave. That's what Sara says, isn't it?*

Thanking the fortune teller, Mary Ellen gets up to leave.

"You are strong, young lady, and you will persevere," says the fortune teller, looking directly into her eyes.

Thanking her again, Mary Ellen turns and bumps into Thaddeus Baird.

"Are you all right, Miss Davis? You look pale." Without waiting for an answer, Thaddeus says, "I believe I'm on your dance card for the last dance. I've come to fetch you." Bowing, he says, "May I have the honor of this dance?"

Shaking off the mood from having her fortune told, Mary Ellen replies, "Of course." She follows Thaddeus onto the dance floor. The Prima Donna Waltz begins, and, gathered in Thaddeus' arms, Mary Ellen follows the dance effortlessly. Mary Ellen, seeking to avoid Thaddeus' gaze, looks around the ballroom, loving the swirl of ladies' skirts and the smooth movement of the mens' feet.

"Are you avoiding looking at me?"

Mary Ellen tilts her head up and smiles. "Of course, not."

"I have spent little time with you, Mary Ellen, and want more. I have something special to ask you. May I meet you at the Jericho School on Friday? It would have to be after my class is over. That would be as your students are leaving. Three o'clock? And, I understand that you will, of course, be chaperoned by Louis."

Mary Ellen only takes a minute to think. She's not sure her parents would approve. "As long as Louis is with me, I believe that would be fine."

Smiling, Thaddeus says, "Wonderful. Until Friday then." Bowing, he adds, "Thank you for the honor."

Mary Ellen is left watching Thaddeus as he makes his way around the ballroom. Shooing away the mixed feelings of euphoria and uncertainty about her parents' feelings toward Thaddeus' invitation, Mary Ellen joins her parents at the door of the ballroom to thank everyone for coming.

***

Later that night, scrunched down in her bed, Mary Ellen remembers the line, "I have something special to ask you." *What special thing could he be asking? Is he proposing?*

Mary Ellen reaches to the bedside table for her journal and a pen. She writes *Mary Ellen and Thaddeus* and draws a heart around the names. On the opposite page, she writes *Mary Ellen Baird* over and over, followed by *Mrs. Thaddeus Baird.* What a delicious secret! For now. Her parents don't need to know, just yet, that she's meeting Thaddeus.

Chapter Thirteen
Mary Ellen Davis

Monday April 23, 1866

Mary Ellen's mother has assigned her the task of cleaning out the mint julep cabinet in the front parlor.

"First of all, you have to empty this cabinet, Miss Mary Ellen. We have to clean the inside, too," says Sara.

Opening the cabinet door, Mary Ellen sees five bottles of bourbon on the bottom shelf of the cabinet. The other two shelves are lined with silver cups. Looking closely, Mary Ellen sees a monogram on the front of each family cup.

"Those cups were passed down from your great-granddaddy. That makes 'em special, so be careful not to scratch them," says Sara.

Unloading the cabinet, Mary Ellen asks, "What is so special about mint juleps? And what is it anyway?"

"It is basically bourbon mixed with sugar poured over ice and topped with crushed mint."

"Sounds horrible. I don't see what all the fuss is about."

"To tell the truth, me either," says Sara.

Looking at the empty cabinet, Mary Ellen asks, "What do we do now?"

Sara hands Mary Ellen a jar of beeswax and a soft cloth. "We wax the cabinet. Put some beeswax on that cloth and rub the wood, but you gotta remember to rub with the grain of the wood. Rub in straight lines. No circles."

Sara watches as Mary Ellen begins polishing the inside of the cabinet. "Miss Mary Ellen, I bet you didn't know—if you write what you wish for in the cabinet, it will come true."

Rocking back on her heels, Mary Ellen looks up at Sara. "Really?"

"Yes, ma'am. That's what your grandmother told me. She also told me she would blister the hide of anyone caught carving on her cabinet."

Mary Ellen is silent, considering what Sara just told her.

When Mary Ellen finishes polishing the cabinet, inside and out, Sara tells her to leave the bourbon bottles where they sit and help her carry the mint julep cups into the kitchen for polishing. A job for another day.

"That cabinet sure does shine. You did good work, Miss Mary Ellen."

"Now, Sara, you're just flattering me, so I'll polish the cabinet next time it needs it." Mary Ellen smiles at Sara, appreciating the praise.

***

The house is quiet. Everyone seems to be asleep. Except for Mary Ellen, who is rolling around in her head what Sara said about the mint julep cabinet: *If you write what you wish for in the cabinet, it will come true.*

So, what would she wish for? A career in journalism? Marriage? No, that's her mother's wish. But what about marriage to Thaddeus? *Yes. Thaddeus. After all, he does have something to ask her.*

Mary Ellen turns back the covers on her bed, slips on her bedroom shoes, and silently makes her way to the kitchen. Inspecting the knives and mixing spoons sticking out of the round glass container on the shelf by the stove, she pulls out a sharp-pointed, thin knife and makes her way to the parlor on tiptoe.

The mint julep cabinet stands empty, just as Mary Ellen and Sara left it. Mary Ellen decides that fewer people will see the carving if it is at the bottom back of the cabinet, behind the bourbon bottles. Lying down flat on her stomach facing the cabinet, Mary Ellen begins to mold letters on the back of the cabinet: *Mary Ellen Davis marries Thaddeus Baird.*

Mary Ellen turns and looks at the antique French clock sitting on the mantle behind her and is shocked to see that over an hour has passed. Looking back at the carving, she decides a date is needed, so she carves today's month and year, *May 1866*. Little does Mary Ellen know that, generations later, relatives will take this as an official marriage date.

Mary Ellen looks at the carving one last time before closing the cabinet doors. *Now, we'll see if grandmother was right and if this wish comes true.*

Chapter Fourteen
Ellen Jones

Thursday, March 22, 1962

It is drizzling rain as Ellen parks Amanda's car across the highway from the Callander plantation house. Opening the car door and stepping out into the rain, Ellen splashes across the highway and bounds up the stairs to her grandfather's house. Looking up at the house with the sharp drops of rain biting at her face, Ellen feels the warm love you feel toward the place you call home.

Even though it is a one-story house, it seems tall with its eight-foot, double front doors and equally tall windows flanked by louvered shutters—green shutters so dark they appear almost black. Opening one of the doors and stepping into the wide hall, Ellen smells the usual coffee and something-good-is-baking smells.

"Granddad?" Ellen yells.

"Back in the dining room," David Henry Callander answers. Ellen walks down the wide hall flanked by huge rooms with very tall ceilings and enters the dining room. She is pleased to find her grandfather alone.

"I've come to pick your brain, Granddad."

"Well, you're welcome to it, child. What's this about?"

"Do I have this right? Your mother, Maude Eleanor Finlayson, and Dad's grandmother, Mary Ellen Davis, were friends?"

Elbow on table, his chin resting in a curled fist, Henry David thinks a moment. "Why, yes, Ellen. Yes, they were."

"What can you remember about Mary Ellen? Anything."

"I remember Mother was in a group with Mary Ellen and two other women who were best friends. They called themselves The Abigails because they were admirers of Abigail Adams."

"So, the Abigails were readers. Educated women?"

"Oh, my goodness, yes. Grandmother Eleanor went to Mississippi College over in Clinton, Mississippi. Rare for a woman to go to college during those days."

"And Mary Ellen?"

"I think she went on to become a journalist. She was bright like the other three. She married a school teacher. Thomas Brown Mitchell. Seems like the two of them did a lot for education around here, especially for underprivileged children."

"So, you don't remember Mary Ellen marrying a Thaddeus Baird, do you?"

"No, absolutely not. If I remember correctly, Thaddeus Baird was at Marion Military Institute. Come to think of it, he died young. Some sort of mystery."

"Really? Oh, gosh, Granddad. Is that true?"

"Best I can remember. I really don't know anything about the man."

"But died young? You're sure?"

"Pretty sure, young lady. I am sorry I don't remember more."

Getting up from the dining room chair, brocaded and probably filled with stains of meals eaten in this wonderful house through the years, Ellen walks around the dining room table and hugs David Henry's neck.

"Thank you, Ellen. And don't be a stranger, hear? Don't forget to come home from that college."

"Oh, Granddad, how could I forget to come back to Callander—and to you and Aunt Zia?"

"That reminds me. Last night, David mentioned Coral Gables. Maybe a job there. Isn't that near your college?"

"Yes. Are you sure? Coral Gables?"

"That's what he said. It is not definite. Just something David is researching. I can hardly stand to think of Zia and David leaving Callander." After a moment, David Henry says, "You have to let your children go. Remember that, Ellen."

Grabbing David Henry by the hand, Ellen attempts to pull him from his chair. "Come on. Walk me to the front door."

***

Ellen's next stop is the Marshall Public Library. She has fond memories of the librarian, Miss Brenda, who helped her find Jonas Stockman, the Revolutionary War soldier buried on Callander land, sorta out in the middle of nowhere. Jonas' tombstone has the usual information engraved on it— name, dates, the fact that he was a Revolutionary War soldier —but it also includes the engraving, "Truth and Honor."

Until recently, Jonas had been a mystery. Why was he buried on Callander land? Zia and Ellen took many walks to Jonas' grave where they stood making up tales about who he was and why he was buried there. It was Miss Brenda who helped Ellen search the library's microfiche for the 1820 Census where they found Jonas. Miss Brenda found Jonas in another library book and discovered Jonas was married with three sons and was a lawyer. There was no explanation for a burial on Callander land.

It was Ellen, cleaning out her grandfather's attic, who found the trunk belonging to Jonas. He had been ostracized by the town for defending an American Indian. Jonas lost his wife and sons and was alone when he died. Ellen's great-great-grandfather admired his honesty and buried him on Callander land.

Ellen found a desk plaque in the trunk with the words "Truth and Honor" engraved on it. She made it her own. It sits on her dorm room desk now. *Truth and Honor.* The phrase has become Ellen's mantra.

***

Miss Brenda is at the circulation desk when Ellen walks into the library. Looking up and seeing Ellen, Miss Brenda claps her hands. She emerges from behind the circulation desk to meet Ellen with a matronly hug. "Ellen, what a day. Some new fiction books came in, and now you are here. How wonderful."

Ellen smiles. "It's wonderful to see you, Miss Brenda."

"And what brings you in today?"

"Trying to get a jump on a story I have to write next week about Jacqueline Kennedy."

"Well, I have some pretty good reference material on her. Come with me."

Ellen watches Miss Brenda check the card catalog, scurry to the reference shelves, and pull out two books on the Kennedys in addition to a green book she hands to Ellen.

"This is the *Reader's Guide to Periodical Literature*. Use it to find articles in *Time* and *Newsweek* and all sorts of magazines. Some of the magazines may be in your university library, if we don't carry them here."

Thanking Miss Brenda, Ellen spreads the material out on a library table and starts to work. After an hour of research, she has scribbled quite a bit of information.

<u>Jacqueline Lee Bouvier Kennedy</u>

Born in Southampton, New York, July 28, 1929.

Named Jacqueline Lee Bouvier.

Father wealthy stockbroker.

Was ten years old when parents divorced. Divorce was rare in 1939 and rarer for a Catholic family like Jackie's.

Jackie was a private person as a child and kept her thoughts to herself.

In 1942, when Jackie was about to turn thirteen, her mother married a businessman named Hugh Auchincloss.

Jackie studied history, literature, art and French at Vassar College and studied in Paris her junior year.

I love this about Jackie. She was a photographer. In the fall of 1951, Jackie was a camera girl for The Washington Times-Herald. *Jackie interviewed people and took pictures of them and wove all this into a newspaper column.*

During this time, Jacqueline met John F. Kennedy, a congressman, and on September 12, 1953, they married at St. Mary's Church in Newport, Rhode Island.

January 1960. John F. Kennedy announced candidacy for presidency.

January 20, 1961. Kennedy became the nation's 35th president. At age 31, Jacqueline Kennedy was the first lady.

Stretching her arms high in the air and interlocking her fingers, Ellen strains to reach even higher. Then, lowering her arms again, she closes the books and magazines and stacks them neatly. It's time to go. After hugging Miss Brenda and thanking her for her help, Ellen heads home.

Chapter Fifteen
Ellen Jones

Saturday, March 24, 1962

Saturday. Ellen's last day at home before going back to Miami and the University of Columbus campus. Ellen is lying in bed ticking off the people she needs to see before flying out in the morning. Jo Jo comes to mind. Ellen wishes more than anything that she could blink and Jo Jo would appear, here at Callander. She misses his strength—the way he supports her.

I know. I'll go see Jo Jo's parents.

Ellen sits up and slides her feet into her worn bedroom slippers. Shuffling to the closet, she picks out a blouse to go with her favorite jeans.

Grabbing her coat off the hook by the back door, Ellen heads for the sharecroppers' cottages. On the walk, she thinks about how she loves this place—Callander. Ellen loves that her grandfather takes care of the people on the land, treating them equally. And she loves that Jo Jo grew up on Callander land, just like she did.

Ellen walks to the batten-board house at the end of the row with its tin roof and porch with the sagging chairs. Jo Jo's mother opens the door before Ellen can knock.

"There you are, Miss Ellen. I just told Mr. Reed I wondered if we'd see you while you were here."

Reaching for Jo Jo's mom's hand, Ellen said, "It's so good to see you. Is Mr. Reed home, too?"

"No. That man is in the fields, even though it's Saturday. He'll be sorry he missed you. Here, sit down with me on the porch. Let's talk a bit."

Ellen turns a ladder-back chair to face Mrs. Reed and waits for her to sit down before asking about Jo Jo.

"What have you heard from Jo Jo?"

"I just got a letter yesterday. He is excited about coming home this summer, but I have a feeling we won't keep him long. He has a real love for that Tripoli place with its old ruins."

"But you know he loves Callander."

"I do know that, and I predict he'll come back to it one day. But now, I think that boy has an itch to be in other places."

"Has he said that?"

"My boy loves the land. He has hinted at helping other countries with their farming. I guess that comes from being in Tripoli."

Ellen remembers the line from a poem Jo Jo wrote to her:

I believe I am an achiever and will travel far.
No one believes that I will see the world
beyond Alabama.

"Oh, Miss Ellen, I'm such a dunderhead. I almost forgot. There's a letter for you in my letter from Jo Jo. Give me a minute to get it."

Ellen hears the door slam behind Jo Jo's mom. She has a minute to sit and look over the land. She sees the soil being turned in preparation for cotton planting, happening in April. Ellen can smell the soil: it is a primordial smell. A dark smell. But the smell of life. It is alive, that soil.

"Here it is," says Mrs. Reed, coming back onto the porch.

Ellen stands up and takes the letter. "Thank you so much," she says. A pause. Then Ellen asks," May I hug you?"

"My goodness, child. Of course, you can."

Ellen leans in and hugs the deceptively strong woman, feeling the sharp shoulder blades through the cotton house dress.

Jo Jo's mom wipes a tear. "Mr. Reed is sure gonna hate he missed you. You come back to see us, Ellen Jones, the next time you're at home."

"I will. I will for sure."

Ellen leaves Mrs. Reed standing on the porch and heads for the one place she wants to read Jo Jo's letter—Jonas Stockman's grave.

Dear Ellen,

I'm writing this on the off chance you will be at Callander when this letter gets to my folks.

I love it when you are on Callander land.

I can just see you walking the fields, talking with your grandfather, and visiting Jonas Stockman's grave. I bet you two cents that if you are reading this letter at Callander, you are at Jonas' grave. Am I right?

We've had some real excitement here at the base. Somebody was here on base with Gus Grissom's flight suit worn during the Mercury flight in July. We all got to try it on. I tell you, I was thrilled. I'm enclosing the picture in this letter.

Bill and Ilenia still plan to have two weddings, one in Tripoli and one when they return stateside this summer. I'd love for you

*to meet them, especially since you and Bill
are both journalists.*

*I'm thinking hard about what I want to do
with my life. I know I want you in it. We'll talk
this summer when I come home.*

*Well, I'm going for now. You know you'll
always be my girl.*

Love,
Jo Jo

Ellen picks up a picture that has fallen out of the envelope. There's square-jawed, handsome Jo Jo in an astronaut's flight suit. He's standing, legs apart, like it's perfectly natural to be in a flight suit for outer space. Ellen heart skips a beat, looking at this man she thinks she loves.

Go to Ellen's Notebook to see Jo Jo's picture.

***

Time to catch up with Essie before Ellen goes back to school. Ellen finds Essie arranging flowers on the dining room table—getting ready for Sunday dinner. Ellen gets a lump in her throat, remembering that she'll fly out in the morning. Thinking she'll miss Sunday dinner with the family.

"Hi, Aunt Essie."

Essie jumps, startled. She turns and smiles to see Ellen. "I knew you'd see me before you fly out in the morning."

Ellen notices that Essie has a fine sheen of sweat on her face. Her face seems to have lost some of its color. "Aunt Essie, are you all right?"

"Of course, I am. Sit down, Ellen. I'll bring us some tea, and we'll talk."

While Essie gets the tea, Ellen takes a close look at the arrangement—a low bowl filled with pink camellias, such beautiful flowers with their glossy green leaves. No matter the season, Essie always has an arrangement on the dining room table in the same low bowl she has used for years.

"Here we go, Ellen," says Essie, handing Ellen a cold glass of tea with a coaster under it. "Now, we haven't talked about going to Lottie's. Whatever do you think about Thaddeus Baird being mean? Doesn't sound like the prince charming we've seen through Mary Ellen's eyes."

"No, I agree. *And* let me tell you about what Grandfather said. I dropped in on him just to see if he remembered hearing anything from that time. You know, David Henry's mother, Maude Eleanor Finlayson, and your grandmother, Mary Ellen Davis, were friends. They were thick as thieves.

When I asked Grandfather if he knew of Thaddeus Baird, he thought he remembered Thaddeus Baird dying young."

"Could that be the answer, Ellen? Could Mary Ellen have married Thaddeus Baird—then he died—and then she married Thomas Brown Mitchell?"

"Maybe. This mystery gets deeper and deeper."

"Well, we'll just keep digging. You'll be back after you finish out your spring semester at school, and we'll have all summer. If we don't find anything before then, maybe we'll find the answer this summer," says Essie.

"I know you're right. We'll solve this. And now I've got to get home. Give me a hug."

Both Essie and Ellen stand up, and Ellen reaches for Essie, hugging her tightly. Essie kisses Ellen on the cheek, then looks her in the eyes and says, "I'll count the days until you get back, girl. You take care at that university."

"Yes, ma'am. And you take care."

On the way home, Ellen thinks about how Essie looked there for a moment, arranging flowers. A worried look arranges itself on Ellen's face. *She'll always have her Aunt Essie, right?*

Chapter Sixteen
Mary Ellen Davis

Friday, April 27, 1866

"Who, What, Where, When, Why and How. That's what you want in the Lead of your news story." Mary Ellen is working with the top two groups of students at the Jericho School—teaching them how to write a news story. She has in the back of her head to produce a newspaper for the class, even if it is just one page. She thinks Mr. Hughes will print it for the students but is holding this news back. She wants the newspaper to be a surprise for the students. First, she needs to make sure Mr. Hughes can print it.

"What's the Lead?" asks Benjamin. "I don't understand."

"The Lead is the opening of your news story—your first paragraph. Let's look at an example. If you saw a bear on your way to school this morning... This bear had two cubs with it. It stood on its hind legs and roared at you before herding its cubs into a nearby cave. The Who would be?"

"Benjamin," says Ruth. "He is the one who saw the bear."

"Yes. Good for you," says Mary Ellen, moving to the blackboard. She erases the board, leaving behind the ghosts of words from other lessons. Speaking to the oldest girl in the class, Mary Ellen asks, "Evelyn, will you come write on the board for us?"

Evelyn is tall for her age and can look eye-to-eye with Mary Ellen. She is a pretty girl who now grins at Mary Ellen. Evelyn loves to be chosen for just about anything as she loves the chance to lead. Moving to the board in her long, flower-sack dress, Evelyn picks up the chalk and prepares to write.

"All right, Evelyn. Please write, 'Who equals Benjamin.'" Then to the students, "And the What? What happened?"

"Benjamin saw a bear," yells John. John is one of the older boys in the class. He rarely speaks during discussion. Ellen nods at John, showing she is pleased to hear John reacting to the story.

"Yes. I think that would be very scary, don't you John?"

John, hangs his head. He is embarrassed for yelling but nods his head in the affirmative.

"And where did this happen?" asks Mary Ellen.

"In the woods. I get it. And the When is this morning on my way to school. I get it. I get it." Benjamin bounces up, clapping his hands together. Evelyn continues to write the answers on the board.

"Yes, you are right." Mary Ellen smiles down at this young boy who has captured her heart. "I know this is confusing but sometimes we do not write out the Why and How. In this case, it is enough to know Who, What, Where, and When in the Lead."

"What about the rest of the story?" asks John.

"After the Lead, we have the Body of the story. The Body of our bear story might describe the bear, tell the reader the bear had two cubs, and disclose that the bear ushered the cubs into a cave. The Why and How may be explained in the Body of the story, if there is a Why and How.

Mary Ellen looks around the school room to see if there are hands raised or quizzical looks on students faces. Seeing none, she says, "In the end, or Conclusion, of the story, I like to tell the reader what will be next in the story. In this case, parents might walk their children to school in case there may be other bear appearances." Evelyn adds this note to the board.

Mary Ellen looks up, satisfied that the children are with her. She continues. "Now, let's begin our first story. I am going to share a story I heard from Mr. Hughes at the newspaper. In case you have not met him, he is a fine gentleman who taught me to write a news story. He owns the *Marshall Times-Standard*."

"So, get comfortable," Ellen motions to the children. "Sit on the floor if you want. But just listen first as I give you the facts as I know them."

She reads from the paper in her hand:

> The Marshall Historical Society honored Loreta Velásquez Saturday night, April 21, 1866, for her service to the Confederate Army. Miss Velásquez was a spy for the Confederate Army. But before she was a spy, she dreamed of being like Joan of Arc.
>
> Velásquez was only fourteen when she married a soldier from Texas who refused to let her accompany him when the Civil War started. Not to be defeated, she had a uniform made, disguised herself as a man with the name Harry T. Buford. As Buford, she raised a group of volunteer soldiers and, with them, traveled to Florida where she found her husband. Only days later, her husband was shot and killed.
>
> Velásquez traveled north and fought at the Battle of Bull Run and the Battle of Ball's Bluff. Returning south, she fought at the Battle of Shiloh. After that, she gave up her uniform to be a spy for the Confederates. Traveling north and locating a friend of her former husband's, she gathered information from the friend to pass on to the Confederacy.

Loreta Velásquez plans to emigrate to Venezuela with her current husband, a Major Wasson.

"A woman dressed as a man?" asked Evelyn.

"She wore pants?" asked Sara.

"She fought with our soldiers?" asked Benjamin.

These questions tumbled over each other as the students responded to Mary Ellen's story. "Yes, yes, and yes," says Mary Ellen. "All true."

Mary Ellen adds, "Now, I want you to write a news story about Loreta Velásquez, but I am going to make it easy. As this is your first story, I am giving you a template to follow. Do you know what a template is?"

Always wanting to please Mary Ellen, Benjamin asks, "A dinner plate for fancy folks?" Snickers in the class follow Benjamin's comment. "That's exactly what I thought, Benjamin." The snickers stopped. "But a template is a pattern to follow or, in our case, an outline to fill in."

Moving to one of the blackboards, Mary Ellen writes:

MY NEWS STORY

THE LEAD

Who:
What:
Where:

When:

Why:

How:

THE BODY

Sentence one:

Sentence two:

Sentence three:

CONCLUSION

"Now, do you think you can write a story about Mrs. Velásquez coming to Marshall?" A chorus of yeses follow her question.

Thomas Brown has been listening to Mary Ellen while working with the abecedarians. Now standing, he walks to face the class. "I think we are a lucky class to have someone with Miss Davis' journalism background to teach us how to write a news story."

Mary Ellen smiles to see the serious nods from the students reacting to Thomas Brown's statement about her. "With your permission, Mr. Mitchell, I'll write the facts about Loreta Velásquez on the empty blackboard. And students," she says turning back toward the eager children,

"I'll expect a news story about Loreta Velásquez's visit to Marshall when I come next Friday."

Thomas Brown says, "Anything you wish, Miss Davis. Anything at all." He stares directly into her eyes. *Is Thomas Brown really flirting with me in front of the class? Oh, my!*

"And now I'll gather my things and go for the day," says Mary Ellen. "If I know Louis, he and Bonnie are waiting impatiently for me outside."

***

Once settled in the buggy, Mary Ellen makes a blowing, huffing noise through her lips, sounding like Bonnie the horse. She is not happy with herself.

I am so fickle! I know I'm attracted to Thaddeus, but what about Thomas Brown? I admit I love it just a little bit when he flirts with me. What to do?

Chapter Seventeen
Ellen Jones

Tuesday, March 27, 1962

Glancing around her dorm room, Ellen takes in the things that uplift her. Things so important to her life. The "Truth and Honor" triangular desk plate that belonged to Jonas Stockman, the books Grandfather Callander had her read to understand prejudice, and the pictures—of Ellen and Jo Jo at the high school prom, of her grandfather walking the fields, of her father and Amanda at their wedding. No picture of Ellen and Luke; the picture of the two of them has long since been safely tucked away in a desk drawer. Out of sight, out of mind.

About Luke in the desk drawer... Ellen had been so very sure she loved Luke. They already had furniture, for gosh sakes, for when they married. It hurts Ellen right between the ribs, thinking about Luke. But why think about Luke?

There is Jo Jo—*Jo Jo who represents home, comfort, support, and probably love.*

Leaving her personal life behind in her dorm room, Ellen heads for the J building. There is a show to produce.

***

As she walks into the studio, Ellen spots Dr. Shelby talking to someone she doesn't know. Dr. Shelby sees Ellen and waves her over.

"Ellen, I am so glad you are back in the fold. Meet Jack Marin, a transfer student from the University. Jack is anchoring today's show. You are directing, right?"

"Number one, I'm glad to be back in the fold, although home was wonderful. Number two, it's good to meet you, Jack." Ellen extends her hand and shakes Jack's hand, giving him a welcoming smile. "Number three, yes, I am directing."

"Oh, Ellen, I really missed you," says Dr. Shelby.

"I missed you, too, Dr. Shelby," Ellen says over her shoulder as she walks into the control room. Today's stories are: Ellen's feature story on Jacqueline Kennedy; one year ago on this date the United States broke off diplomatic relations with Cuba; and Archbishop Rummel ends race segregation in New Orleans Catholic schools.

Ellen takes her place as director and welcomes the technical director, who switches between camera shots, and the audio technician. Putting on her headphones, Ellen speaks to the floor director in the studio. "Okay, kids. We need anchors and cameramen in their places."

Ellen watches Jack Marin take his place alongside the infamous Sandra. After sound checks and a quick check with her control room crew, the countdown begins. On Ellen's cue, the floor director cues the anchors.

"Good evening and welcome to *Miami News Now*. I'm Sandra Rowen."

"And I'm Jack Marin. Before she was our most-photographed first lady, Jackie Kennedy was behind the camera. Here's Ellen Jones with the story."

Ellen cues her edited package on the first lady as a photographer and listens to the voiceover.

"The beautiful, young photographer could be any photographer on the streets of New York. Stylish but professional black dress, short bobbed hair, camera with flash attachment held at the ready…"

Ellen watches objectively as her story rolls. Jackie Bouvier and her camera. Jackie Bouvier attending the coronation of Queen Elizabeth. Ellen bites the inside of her cheek, she's so excited. She breathes deeply as she instructs camera two to get a close-up of Sandra.

Sandra delivers the story about Cuba on camera two. Then Jack delivers the story on Archbishop Rummel on camera one.

After the show, Dr. Shelby approaches Ellen. "Great story, Ellen. And great show. So, what is it going to be? Reporter or director?"

"I love directing, Dr. Shelby, but there is nothing like researching a subject, interviewing its participants, writing and editing the story. I don't want to give that up."

Jack enters the conversation. "You know, I remember the United States breaking off diplomatic relations with Cuba. My family has lived in Miami for years, but I have grandparents and a lot of other relatives in Cuba."

"Then you and Ellen need to get together. This girl went into Cuba and rescued her Aunt Zia who lived in Havana at the time," says Dr. Shelby.

"That's true?" asks Jack.

"'Fraid so. Aunt Zia was accidently caught up in a conspiracy to kill Castro and was imprisoned in La Cabaña. Uncle David got her released and took her to friends near Santiago. When I was on vacation in Montego Bay with the broadcasting crew, Uncle David arranged for me to go with a fisherman friend of his to Santiago, pick up Aunt Zia, and bring her back to Montego Bay and on to the States."

"That's hard to believe. Sounds terrifying," says Jack.

"Believe you me, it was," says Ellen. "My uncle is in the states now with Aunt Zia, but he only came after his daughter died and his son, Julio, came here with the Pedro Pan Movement. His daughter, Carlota, died of pneumonia while working with the Literacy Movement."

"Well, we definitely need to get together and talk about our Cuba connections. But now, I've gotta run to calculus class. My grade is so low in that class, I can't miss a minute. Bye, director lady. See you soon."

The corners of Dr. Shelby's eyes crinkle with amusement as he watches Ellen watch Jack leave the broadcasting studio. *Surely Ellen won't fall for another anchor!*

See Ellen's Notebook for the complete story on Jacqueline Kennedy, tips on writing a feature story, and scriptwriting using a split-page format.

***

Leaving the J building for her dorm, thoughts are flitting through Ellen's mind like the fuzzy ends of dandelions blowing in the wind. *Who is Jack, and what is her first impression of him?* Aunt Zia's story had shocked him, she could tell. There was still so much happening in Cuba.

When Ellen thinks of Cuba, she thinks immediately of Mr. Chenard, her Cuban-exile friend who works at the

Coral Gables Police Department as a janitor. Mr. Chenard once taught literature at the University of Havana. He rebelled when Castro dictated what literature he could teach students: all Castro's recommended works had a Marxist bent.

Leaving behind his beloved wife, Louisa, Mr. Chenard had escaped to Miami in a small boat. He could have been imprisoned or killed if caught. Why did he leave Cuba? Louisa's family is friendly with the Cuban president. Mr. Chenard was actively rebelling against Castro and knew if he was captured it would harm Louisa and her family. He left the country he loved to protect the woman he loved.

Ellen, on the way to her dorm, changes directions on a sudden impulse and heads for the bus line that will take her to Coral Gables. Remembering Mr. Chenard works a full day on Tuesday, she plans to catch him while he is still at the police station.

On the bus ride to the police station, Ellen thinks of her previous visits. Her first visit was a professional one: she interviewed the detective in charge of a robbery investigation—a robbery at one of the older, more influential homes of Coral Gables. Mr. Chenard had been in the interview room, emptying the trash. Ellen and Mr. Chenard had discovered their mutual connection to Cuba.

Since that initial visit, Ellen and Mr. Chenard met often, mostly on Friday afternoons. From those meetings had come a lasting friendship—and a Peabody Award for the story Ellen had produced on Mr. Chenard's life in Cuba.

Ellen pulls the rope to indicate to the bus driver that she wants to get off on Salzedo Street, where the Coral Gables Police and Fire Department building is located. The building dominates the block. Walking in, Ellen is thrilled to see Police Desk Sergeant Baker at the reception desk.

"Well, a sight for sore eyes you are, young lady," says Sergeant Baker.

"You, too, Sergeant. So good to see you. Is Mr. Chenard around?" asks Ellen.

"I believe he is. Should be ready for his break soon. When was the last time you saw Mr. Chenard?"

"December. I remember going to a Cuban party with him in December."

"Well, you probably don't know Mr. Chenard's big news."

"What? Does it involve Cuba?"

"It's his story to tell, young lady. You'll have to wait and let him tell you. Hold on. I'll tell him he has a visitor. Better yet, follow me. We'll surprise him."

Ellen follows Sergeant Baker down the hall where conference rooms are located. Mr. Chenard, elegant as usual, is coming out of the last room. He sees Ellen and stops. Taking in her appearance a smile breaks out on his face, and he flings his arms wide. Ellen steps into his arms.

"Hija. Estoy contento de verte."

"I'm glad to see you, Mr. Chenard. Do you have a minute to talk?"

"I always have time for you, young lady. It's warm. Let us go sit in the little park across the street." Saying her good-byes to Sergeant Baker, Ellen follows Mr. Chenard to the park where they sit on the closest bench.

"I want to know all that is going on with your wonderful family," he says as they settle on the park bench. "And if you want to talk about your love life, we can do that, too."

"Maybe we'll talk about that, but Sergeant Baker tells me you have big news. He won't tell me what it is."

"Oh, I do have big news. The best news ever. Louisa is coming to Miami. You may remember we secretly exchange letters though a friend at the University of Havana. The Cuban president is sending Louisa's father to Miami for a business meeting, and her father is bringing the entire family with him. Louisa assures me she can get away and come to me. She will not go back to Cuba."

"I'm ecstatic for you."

"You know Louisa holds my heart. If she comes to me, I will be whole."

Ellen smiles at this romantic, beautiful man. "When does she arrive?"

"Tomorrow! Can you believe it? She is coming tomorrow. The family will be staying at the Fontainebleau —only the best for Louisa's father."

"But how will you meet her?"

"We are to meet at the bottom of the famous floating staircase at seven o'clock on Thursday morning."

"Your love story is more beautiful than any of the love stories I've read in novels, Mr. Chenard."

"Please pray for us, Ellen. Tomorrow. I can hardly believe it."

"I will pray for you both. But I know the next time I see you, Louisa will be with you. I can hardly wait to meet her."

"Enough about me. What about you?"

"I am helping Aunt Essie solve a mystery. My ancestor supposedly married one man in May of 1866 and another in December of that same year. It's quite the mystery."

"And your young man, Luke?" Ellen frowns for a moment. Then she remembers Mr. Chenard would have no way of knowing about Luke.

"Luke and I are no longer together. He cheated on his Peabody Award submission by stealing my Aunt Zia's work. I could never be in a relationship with him after that."

"I am so sorry, Ellen. It is very difficult to love someone and discover you don't really know them. But what about that boy back home?"

"Jo Jo? I'm pretty sure he is the one. He is coming home this summer. I will know for sure when I see him." Ellen stands up, brushes off her skirt, and smiles at Mr. Chenard. "Now, I have to get back to the dorm and study. It has been wonderful to spend time with you."

"If you must leave me, let me walk you to the bus stop. One day I will have a Rolls Royce, and you will not have to ride the bus."

"I look forward to that. When you get that Rolls Royce, you can drive me all the way to Marshall to meet my family."

"Consider it done. And Louisa will be with us."

Chapter Eighteen
Ellen Jones

Thursday, March 29, 1962

Ellen has just arrived at the broadcasting studio. Looking through the windows into Dr. Shelby's office, she freezes. Luke is in Dr. Shelby's office. He hasn't changed—blue eyes, handsome, dark hair coiling along his neck. It seems so natural to see him there. Talking with Dr. Shelby. Owning the space around him.

Jack walks up, and, standing beside Ellen, notices where she is looking. "Is this the Luke I've heard so much about? Luke the Legend?"

Ellen cannot speak. She simply nods her head.

"I know what happened with the Peabody story. That must have been horrible for you."

Ellen nods her head again.

"If it helps, I lost someone, too. We were to be married. Until she eloped with one of our broadcasting teachers."

This gets Ellen's attention. "That's why you transferred?"

"Yes. I just couldn't be in that broadcasting program everyday with everyone feeling sorry for me."

Ellen smiles at Jack. "Well, that's just our good luck. You did a fine job of anchoring the other day."

"Thank you. That's what I want to do with my life. I know I'll have to start at a small station and work my way up, but that's okay. I'll get to a major market one day."

Ellen is taken aback by what Jack just said. So different from Luke who bragged about going into a major market right out of college and taking Ellen with him. She can't help but compare the two. From what she's seen, Jack is just as good at his craft as Luke, but he has a humility Luke has never had.

Dr. Shelby and Luke walk out of Dr. Shelby's office, still talking. Looking up, Luke spots Ellen. Dr. Shelby, aware Luke has stopped talking, looks up and sees Ellen with Jack. It is awkward, but Dr. Shelby nudges Luke in Ellen's direction.

"Luke is here to get his transcript from the registrar's office, and he stopped by to see me. I'm so glad he did. Luke, you haven't met Jack. Jack Marin, Luke O'Neal. Jack has taken your place at the anchor desk, Luke."

Luke takes a moment to observe Jack. Stepping forward, Luke extends his hand. "So nice to meet you, Jack. You couldn't work with a better group of broadcasters."

"Yes," says Jack. "I'm discovering that."

Turning to Ellen, Luke says, "Ellen, will you walk me out?" All eyes are on Ellen. Even the students working on scripts in the main room are watching the drama unfold. Ellen nods and follows Luke out of the J building. Outside, Luke stops and turns to Ellen. He tries for humor, but it falls flat. "Is Jack taking my place with you as well?"

Angry, Ellen clinches her fists. "How beneath you, Luke."

"Yes, I suppose you are right. I just miss you so much." Luke stops talking and stares at Ellen like he is memorizing every square inch of her. "Is there any chance for us? I'm working hard at the *Atlanta Journal*, and they like my work. I should be able to enroll in the program at the University of Alabama in the fall."

Ellen can't help but smile at Luke's optimism. Luke is supposed to work at the *Journal* for a year before they recommend him to the University. Encouraged by Ellen's smile, Luke takes a step toward Ellen. Ellen takes a step backward.

"Luke, I've tried to hate you. I think Aunt Zia has forgiven you. She says I should, too. I am trying. I really don't hate you, Luke."

He throws his arms up in the air and shouts, "Hallelujah." Several students walking by take notice and laugh. The old Luke is back.

"But I cannot be in a relationship with you, Luke. I just can't."

All the exuberance drains from Luke. "I have no hope?"

"No, but we can be friends. I wish the best for you. I want to see you anchoring a news show someday."

"And you will, Ellen. About the friendship, I'll take it." Luke leans over and kisses Ellen on the mouth. "Just friends," he says.

Ellen turns and walks away.

Bittersweet! That's what she feels about Luke. The joy of planning a wedding. The gut-wrenching feeling of resentment and hurt when he stole Zia's story. The Fifties song, "You Cheated, You Lied," runs through Ellen's head more than she'd like to admit. But she is surprised to find she is moving on. She can be friends with Luke. Not Luke the Legend. Just Luke.

***

When Ellen passes through the dorm doors, she hears the phone ringing. Rushing to the wooden phone booth on her hall, Ellen grabs the receiver before the ringing stops. It is her dad. She has a premonition of bad news—a tightening, cramping in her gut.

"I've got bad news," Will says.

Ellen bites the joint on her thumb. She is silent.

"Ellen, are you there?"

Finally, Ellen says, "Yes, Dad. I'm here."

"Essie is in the hospital in Selma. She had a heart attack. She was in the kitchen at the Mitchell House. Lila, Granddaddy Callander's maid, went over to take some greens to Essie and found her on the kitchen floor."

Ellen can't speak. The tightening in her gut seems to spread over her entire body.

"Ellen? Are you hearing me? Ellen?"

"How bad is she, Dad?" Ellen asks in a soft voice.

"We'll know more tomorrow. But you'll be here tomorrow. I have you on a flight at 8:30 a.m. on Southern Airlines. Get to the airport early to get your tickets."

Ellen begins crying. Will listens, giving her some time.

"Okay, Dad. I'll be on that flight in the morning."

"Ellen, I have faith. Essie will come home from the hospital and will be taking care of everyone before we know it."

"I'm sure you're right, Dad. It's just such a shock."

"I know, Sug. Now, I will see you in the morning. Love you."

"Love you, too, Dad."

Chapter Nineteen
Ellen Jones

Friday, March 30, 1962
Saturday, March 31, 1962

Dr. Shelby had insisted on driving Ellen to the airport when she told him about Aunt Essie. Now he walks with Ellen to the Southern Airlines ticket counter.

"Are you holding a ticket to Mobile for Ellen Jones?"

Turning to search the counter behind her, the attendant searches and turns back around, ticket in hand. "Yes, I have it right here."

Ellen asks the attendant if she needs to see identification. The attendant assures her she doesn't. It crosses Ellen's mind that anyone could claim her ticket, if they wanted to fly to Mobile. Ellen thanks the attendant and turns to say good-bye to Dr. Shelby.

Before she can speak, Dr. Shelby says, "I'll walk you to the gate, Ellen." On their way to the gate, he comments on

Ellen's attire. "I think this is the first time I've seen you wearing a suit with a hat and gloves."

"It may be the only time you see me like this." Ellen smiles at Dr. Shelby.

Flying is a luxurious affair—like going to an up-scale restaurant—and the people flying dress accordingly. The men wear suits and ties. The females wear suits or dresses with hats and often gloves. Ellen is wearing a royal blue knit suit with a skirt that falls below the knees. Her head is topped with a white, fluffy affair—a pillbox hat made of feathers.

Later, cocktails and wine will be served on the house along with a fancy multi-course meal that will likely include soup, salad, meat, vegetables, and dessert. Sometimes the main course is lobster. Ellen will abstain from the wine, knowing her father would probably not approve of a tipsy Ellen getting off the plane in Mobile. The service, provided by the stewardesses, is always impeccable. Ellen has noticed on previous flights that the stewardesses are all very attractive, and she thinks they must be hired for their looks. Ellen is not wrong. There is an age and weight limit for stewardesses, and they cannot be married. They most certainly cannot have children.

Arriving at her gate, Ellen turns to Dr. Shelby. "Thank you for caring, Dr. Shelby. And thank you for bringing me to the airport."

"Of course, I am always happy to help my students. Let us know how your aunt is faring. All of us at the broadcasting department are concerned."

"I promise. And thank you again." Ellen turns, climbs the steps, and enters the plane.

Dr. Shelby muses that he has never had a student like Ellen. No doubt she will be a success in life.

***

The Edmund Pettus Bridge soars over the Alabama River and into Selma. Sitting in the back seat, Ellen barely notices crossing it onto Broad Street. Ellen sees shoppers walking down Broad Street; they are not in a hurry. How can they continue to shop while Essie is in the hospital? Why hasn't the world stopped for them, like it has for Ellen?

Pulling into the hospital parking lot, Will walks around the car and opens the door for Amanda and then Ellen, who is seated in the back. "Come on, Sug," Will says to Ellen. "Your Aunt Essie is going to be okay. Now, don't go in her hospital room looking like gloom and doom."

They head through the hospital front doors, cross the lobby, and ride the elevator to the third floor. Will knows where to go. Room 304. Ellen stops for a moment behind Will and Amanda. She holds her breath, then lets it go with a whoosh when she sees a man standing over Essie holding her hand. A handsome man with an elongated, olive-toned face and dark hair slicked back from his forehead. He is dressed in dark gray pants, a traditional white dress shirt, and a skinny, red knit tie.

The man looks up as the three walk in and, without waiting for Essie to introduce him, says, "Hello. I am assuming you are Louise's family."

Louise?

"I am Nicholas Ellard. So pleased to finally meet you." He walks around Essie's bed and extends his hand. "Oh, I am assuming you are Will and Amanda." Mystified, Will and Amanda shake his hand.

At this point, Essie interjects, "Nicholas and I have been friends for a few years. I'm sorry you have not met him before."

Met him before? How about knowing he existed before? Will is thinking what Amanda is thinking. Ellen would be thinking the same had Aunt Essie not mentioned her secret on her trip home weeks before.

"And, of course, this is our Ellen, Nick."

Nicholas turns to Ellen. "You are just the way Louise described you. So nice to finally meet you."

Coming to life, Ellen realizes this is the "drop-dead gorgeous" man Essie had talked about earlier. Ellen smiles at Nicholas. "So nice to meet you, too."

Essie speaks up, scolding Ellen in a pissy way. "Ellen, why aren't you in Miami? You shouldn't be here."

"Do you think I am going to let you have a heart attack without me?" answers Ellen in the same pissy manner. Essie falls back on her pillow laughing.

"Seriously, I am okay, and you should be at school."

Ellen tears up. "I was worried about you, Aunt Essie. Had to see you for myself." Ellen leans over and gingerly kisses Essie on the check.

"I love you, child. But everything really is okay. My cardiologist says I can go home in the morning. How long are you here?"

"I told my professors I'd be back in class on Tuesday if all went well."

"Good. You can save my reputation by staying with me at the Mitchell House. Nick was insisting he stay and take care of me. Can you imagine the tongue-wagging that would cause?"

"I'll be glad to stay." Ellen grins. "Have to protect your stellar reputation."

"Well, with that problem solved, I need to get to the bank. Wonderful to meet all of you, and thank you, Ellen, for taking care of my girl," says Nicholas. Nicholas makes his exit to dropped jaws. Turning to Essie, expecting answers, they find her softly snoring.

***

Saturday afternoon finds Essie dozing in the parlor while Ellen is on her way upstairs. She hears a soft knock at the front door. Walking back to the door, Ellen peers through the sidelights. The cranberry glass distorts the image in front of the door, but Ellen is pretty sure it's a woman. Soft knock again.

Ellen opens the door to find Miss Lottie—thin, wrinkled Miss Lottie with wisps of hair that have escaped from her tight bun and are blowing across her cherry face. Ellen's impression is that Miss Lottie has just walked up the front steps to the Mitchell House, as she is huffing, trying to catch her breath. A basket is hanging from her left arm and she reaches across to rearrange the napkin covering the basket.

"Miss Lottie, I'm delighted to see you, but are you all right?"

"Fine, fine, Miss Ellen. Just need to catch my breath."

"Please come in. Aunt Essie is right here in the parlor. Come sit."

Rousing from her nap, Essie spots Lottie. Her quick breath of surprise gives way to pleasure at seeing Lottie again. "Well, Lottie, how good to see you," says Essie.

"I heard you were in that hospital in Selma and had to see for myself you were all right."

"How nice of you, Lottie. But as you can see, I'm fine."

Lottie sits the basket down on the floor and removes a glass jar filled with sepia-colored liquid.

"I brought you some of my almond tea." Reaching into the basket, Lottie removes another glass jar. "And I brought you some of my cherry wine, left over from last year. It's just the ticket to perk you up."

Essie laughs. "Yes, I imagine it is. Now, you've got to sit down and visit, Lottie."

"Yes," says Ellen. "Sit with us for a while."

"I believe I will," says Lottie. Settling down on the velvet sofa, she says, "I wanted to make sure those doctors fixed you up. And another thing—you were asking about Mary Ellen, and I remembered two things I want to pass on before they pass right out of this old brain."

Essie slides up to the edge of her chair. Ellen sits up straight.

"First, there was some sort of scandal about Mary Ellen. As best I can recall, it was about something that she did before she married Thomas Brown Mitchell. The kitchen staff at the time was gossiping about it. I've tried and tried, and that's all I can remember."

"That's okay," says Ellen. "Don't worry."

Essie, always to the point, asks, "And the second thing?"

"This may not mean anything to you, but I—loving a mystery like I do—like to think about it." Essie and Ellen wait while Lottie fidgets with her dress hem.

"Lottie?"

"There is supposed to be a secret drawer somewhere in this house. My guess is it is in this very parlor we're sitting in."

"How do you know this, Lottie?" asks Essie.

"I got it from the horse's mouth. Mr. Davis was telling Mrs. Davis and Mary Ellen about it over breakfast one morning. They didn't know I was around. Probably wouldn't have cared. But I kept quiet. The idea strikes my fancy, and I never have forgotten it."

"Did great-great-grandaddy Davis know where the secret drawer is?" asks Ellen.

"He did not say. I don't think he knew." Rising, Lottie says, "Now, I gotta get back down your front steps to the road. I hitched a ride with that Marshall Bennett, and he'll leave me if I'm not waiting at the foot of the steps on time."

Ellen stands up to see Lottie to the front door. "You keep your seat, Miss Essie. Your beautiful Ellen will see me out. You take care now, you hear?"

"I will Lottie. Please come back." Essie smiles. "And bring some more of your cherry wine with you."

Lottie slaps her leg and laughs out loud.

"You won't do, Miss Essie. You just won't do."

Ellen follows Lottie out the front door and onto the porch. Sure enough, Marshall Bennett is waiting in his wagon at the bottom of the steps. Ellen waves. He tips his hat. Ellen watches as Miss Lottie takes one step at a time to reach the wagon.

Walking back into the parlor, Ellen is not surprised to see Essie inspecting the small table near the chair she favors. Looking up at Ellen, Essie chortles. For the first time since Ellen's arrival, Essie is animated and excited.

"Ellen, just imagine. A secret drawer."

"And even more interesting—Mary Ellen was involved in a scandal?"

Chapter Twenty
Mary Ellen Davis

Friday, May 11, 1866

Mary Ellen is working with the middle group of students at the Jericho School, but her mind is not on Phyllis Wheatley's "Hymn to the Evening." It's a beautiful poem, but all she can think of is her meeting with Thaddeus after school today.

Finally, Thomas Brown announces class is dismissed. Mary Ellen moves to the front doors where she can wish the students good-bye and is surprised to see Thaddeus entering the back of the old Garvey mansion. Margaret Bell is visiting the school today, and, as Thomas Brown is engaged in discussion with Mrs. Bell, Mary Ellen leaves without wishing him a good afternoon. Mary Ellen walks briskly to the buggy where Louis is waiting.

"Louis, I need just a moment with Mr. Baird. He just walked into the old house. I will be back shortly."

127

"Miss Mary Ellen, I don't like this. You don't need to be alone with no man."

"Oh, Louis, don't be a fuddy duddy. I will be right back."

Mary Ellen turns and walks into the Garvey mansion before Louis can object further. She enters a wide hall that runs front to back of the house. Surprisingly, someone has left furniture, albeit dusty and clothed with cobwebs, in the wide hall. Mary Ellen takes in a secretary desk, its top half filled with leather books. She notices a fainting couch, along with a desk and chair, before spotting Thaddeus half-way down the hall.

"Mary Ellen, you came." Thaddeus walks to Mary Ellen and takes both her hands in his. "If I know Louis, he doesn't like you in here with me, so I'll be quick. I like you, Mary Ellen, and I want to enter a pre-engagement period with you."

"A pre-engagement period?" says Mary Ellen, her voice a little shaky.

"Yes," says Thaddeus. "We would get to know each other while remaining faithful to each other." To Mary Ellen's amazement, Thaddeus pulls a velvet-wrapped ring out of his pocket. Folding back the velvet, Mary Ellen sees a gold ring set with three sapphires. "This was my grandmother's. The three stones represent the past, the present, and the future."

So taken aback is Mary Ellen, she just stands there, looking at Thaddeus.

"Well, Mary Ellen, if you accept, hold out your right hand."

Mary Ellen obliges, staring at her hand as he slides the ring on her finger.

Thaddeus puts his hand under her chin, tilting her head up toward his dark eyes. "I have been dreaming of this since I first sat by you in your family dining room."

Thaddeus bends his head and kisses Mary Ellen, gently at first. Mary Ellen begins to pull back, but Thaddeus puts his hand behind her head, forcing her mouth against his and biting her lip.

Mary Ellen struggles. She feels her dress ripping. Thaddeus' other hand is squeezing her breast brutally. Wrenching her mouth away from his, Mary Ellen screams and screams and screams. Even when Louis runs into the hallway, Mary Ellen keeps screaming.

Louis is fully aware of Thaddeus' actions and grabs both Thaddeus' arms and twists them behind his back, holding them tightly as he says, "Miss Mary Ellen, I need you to go get in the buggy now." Mary Ellen just stares at Louis. Louis has his hands full, holding the squirming Thaddeus. "Miss Mary Ellen," Louis shouts. "Go get in the buggy!"

Mary Ellen takes in Louis holding a furious Thaddeus. She looks at Thaddeus and then down at the ring on her finger. She looks him straight in the eye, removes the ring, and throws it at him. She darts for the doorway to the old mansion and runs to the buggy.

In a perfect world, she gets in the buggy, and Louis drives her home. But no. As Mary Ellen reaches the buggy, Margaret Bell and Thomas Brown walk out of the schoolhouse. Mary Ellen feels their eyes on her, taking in her bruised lip, mussed hair, and torn dress.

A furious Thaddeus Baird hurries out of the mansion, gets in his buggy, and drives off without a glance in anyone's direction. Louis emerges slowly from the mansion, making eye contact with Thomas Brown. "I will be taking Miss Mary Ellen home now," he says. Louis gets in the buggy, turns it around, and heads down the driveway, leaving a stunned Margaret Bell and Thomas Brown behind.

***

Luckily, Mary Ellen's parents are not at home when she and Louis arrive back at Revival House. Mary Ellen remains sitting in the buggy when Louis pulls up in front of the house. She is not responding to his questions. Louis is terrified and goes into the house to fetch Sara, who comes running.

Sara crawls up inside the buggy beside Mary Ellen and, taking Mary Ellen's hand in hers, pats her hand, trying to get her attention. Mary Ellen turns to look at Sara. Tears begin to trickle down her face. Sara tucks a stray strand of hair behind Mary Ellen's ear, and says, "Come on in the house, Miss Mary Ellen."

Between Louis and Sara, they get Mary Ellen into the kitchen and seated at the kitchen table. Leaving for a moment, Sara returns with Mr. Davis' brandy bottle.

"Miss Mary Ellen, I'm pouring you a little of your daddy's brandy. You look like you need it. Then maybe you can tell Sara what happened." Mary Ellen sips the brandy but doesn't talk.

Sara turns to Louis. "What in the world? What do you know about this?"

"After school today, Miss Mary Ellen sees that Thaddeus Baird going in the old Garvey house, and she follows him inside. I tell her not to go in that house with that man, but she won't listen. Before I know it, she's screaming. I tell you, my heart goes to my feet. When I run in the house, that Thaddeus is attacking Miss Mary Ellen. She's screaming to beat the band."

He takes a quick breath, then continues. "I convinced her to go get in the buggy while I held Mr. Baird off. But the really bad news is Miss Margaret Bell and Mr. Mitchell both witnessed her torn dress and messed up hair as she came out of the house. Mr. Baird stomped out right after her and left in a fury. You know that Margaret Bell will talk. Lawdy, Miss Mary Ellen is ruined."

Mary Ellen puts her head down on the kitchen table and sobs.

"Hush, Louis. Let me think," says Sara. After a moment, Sara says, "The first thing we gotta do is get Miss Mary Ellen upstairs. Miss Mary Ellen, you need to change your dress and fix your hair before your mother gets home. Now, come on."

In the bedroom, Sara helps Mary Ellen change her dress. "Miss Mary Ellen, you need to understand I'm not trying to hide this from your parents. They need to know what happened to you. I just think it's better if you face them in a clean dress. And you gotta be the one to tell them. No one else, you hear?"

"They'll blame me, and they'll blame Louis," says Mary Ellen, softly. "It's my fault. I can't stand for them to blame Louis."

"Humph. That fool should have never allowed you to go in that house, Miss Mary Ellen."

"It's not his fault, Sara. Louis couldn't stop me. I was determined to hear what Mr. Baird had to tell me."

"In my mind, what it boils down to is this: it's Thaddeus Baird's fault. That weasel."

"Yes, Sara. I agree that he's a weasel. How could I be so infatuated with him? Am I crazy?"

"No, Miss Mary Ellen. You just had a bad experience with love. We all have that at one time or another." Sara leans over, kisses Mary Ellen on the forehead, and leaves the bedroom.

***

The family gathers for a supper of leftover pork chops, green beans, and sweet potatoes. They are listening to Adam talk about the latest idea he has for his upcoming birthday.

"This is it. If you give me this, I'll not ask for another thing," says Adam.

"What is it now?" asks Mr. Davis.

"A banjo. And not just any banjo. I want a five-string banjo."

"And you know how to play a banjo?" asks Mrs. Davis.

"Well, no. But Mr. Harvey plays. If he can teach Mary Ellen to play the piano, he can teach me to play a banjo."

Adam looks at Mary Ellen, expecting a response. Puzzled when he finds Mary Ellen staring off into space, Adam says, "Anyone who can teach Doodle to play a piano can work miracles." Still no response from Mary Ellen.

By now, the entire family is looking at Mary Ellen.

"Mary Ellen, are you not feeling well?" asks Mrs. Davis.

"No, Mother. Please excuse me from supper." Without waiting for permission, Mary Ellen slides back her chair and leaves the table.

"Now, what on earth…?" asks Mr. Davis.

"Let's finish supper, and I'll check on her," says Mrs. Davis.

"Fine, Mother. This is not like Mary Ellen. Make sure you check on her."

At that moment, Mrs. Davis notices Sara, who stares after Mary Ellen with a worried look. *What on earth, indeed!* thinks Mrs. Davis as she rushes to finish her supper.

Chapter Twenty-One
Mary Ellen Davis

Monday, May 14, 1866

Entering the kitchen before breakfast, Mary Ellen hears her mother tell Sara that Margaret Bell is visiting that morning. "I have no idea why she's visiting me. She probably has founded a new committee she wants me to join. I'm going to be firm and tell her no."

Sara looks at Mary Ellen who is gripping the back of a kitchen chair like she is preventing the chair from running away. Sara frowns at Mary Ellen and nods at Mrs. Davis. After giving Sara a look that says "I will," Mary Ellen sits down in the kitchen chair she had been gripping so fiercely.

"Mother, I know why Mrs. Bell is coming to visit."

"Oh, did she mention it to you at church?"

"No, ma'am."

"Well, you want to tell me how you know?"

"She is coming to tell you I was in a compromising position at school last Friday."

"What?" says Mrs. Davis, turning from the cup of tea she is preparing.

Mary Ellen looks at Sara for support; Sara nods her head and smiles.

"I meant to tell you Friday but just couldn't. I'm worried about Louis. If I tell you, you have to promise me right now you and Daddy won't punish Louis."

"What's this about not punishing Louis?" says Mr. Davis, as he walks into the kitchen tying his tie.

Facing her father, Mary Ellen says, "I was involved in something awful at school Friday. In no way was it Louis' fault. As a matter of fact, he saved me. I want your promise you won't punish him. Then, I'll tell what happened and why Mrs. Bell is visiting Mother this morning."

"I don't usually make this type of promise, Mary Ellen, but I see how strongly you feel about Louis' role in whatever happened. I agree, and I'm sure your mother will agree. We will not punish Louis."

After taking a sip of tea, Mrs. Davis nods her agreement.

"Now, what happened?" asks Ellen's dad.

"Thaddeus Baird told me he had something to ask me and wanted to know if I would meet him after school on Friday. Curious, I told him I would as long as Louis was with us. When I walked out the school door Friday, I saw

Mr. Baird entering the old Garvey house. Louis was waiting in the buggy. I told Louis to stay in the buggy, that I was just going to go in the house for a minute. Louis was really upset, but I walked off before he could follow me."

"My Lord, Mary Ellen! You went in that house alone?"

"Yes, ma'am. Mr. Baird told me he wanted us to be pre-engaged, and he put his grandmother's ring on my finger." Mary Ellen starts to cry. She can't stand the shocked look on her mother's face.

Minutes pass. *I can't do this. I can't just sit here and cry.* Then, looking up at her parents, Mary Ellen says, "That's not all."

"That's not enough?" asks her mother. "Unchaperoned and alone with a man?"

"He attacked me," says Mary Ellen quietly. I screamed and screamed. Louis saved me.

"Oh, my Lord," says Mary Ellen's mother, sitting down in the nearest chair.

"When I ran out of the house to get in the buggy, Mrs. Bell, who had been visiting the school, and Mr. Mitchell saw me. My dress was torn, and I was crying. They then saw Mr. Baird run to his carriage and drive off."

Without thinking, Mrs. Davis says, "You're ruined, Mary Ellen." And she begins to cry. "How am I going to face Mrs. Bell?"

"I'll tell you how you are going to face Mrs. Bell. With the truth and with your head held high," says Mr. Davis. Turning to look at Mary Ellen, Mr. Davis adds, "You don't have to do this, Mary Ellen, but I'll respect you if you face Mrs. Bell with your mother."

"I am going to kill the son of a bitch," Mr. Davis says, walking out of the room.

***

"Would you like tea, Mrs. Bell?" asks Sara. She invites Mrs. Bell into the ladies' parlor.

"Thank you, no, Sara. I won't be here long."

At that point, Mrs. Davis, followed by Mary Ellen, comes into the parlor. Mrs. Bell's jaw drops. She's surprised to see Mary Ellen.

"We're delighted to see you, Mrs. Bell. Are you sure we can't offer you something?"

"No, as I told Sara, this will be a short visit."

Waiting until she's settled in her chair, Mrs. Davis asks, "And how can we help you today, Margaret?"

"I think it is more of a matter of me helping you. I think it is my Christian duty to tell you your daughter was in the old Garvey house alone with Mr. Thaddeus Baird, and she came out of the house crying. Her dress was torn, and her hair—well, her hair was all messed up. Not proper. Not proper at all. Again, my Christian duty forces me to tell you the kind of daughter you are raising. It appears she is a slut."

Sara is frozen by the door. *Miss Mary Ellen a slut? How dare the woman?*

Mrs. Davis stands up from her chair.

Here it comes! thinks Sara.

"I will tell you the kind of daughter I am raising," says Mrs. Davis, both hands on her hips. "I'm raising a solid A student in school who wants to be a journalist. She writes stories that are published in the *Times-Standard*, and she volunteers at Mr. Mitchell's school on Fridays, helping those students. I'm raising an honest daughter who loves God and her family. How dare you call this precious child a slut for defending herself against a brutal attack by that Thaddeus Baird."

Ellen's mother has not moved, and she is not finished yet. "If anyone is a slut, Margaret, it's you. Didn't you steal Martha Bunn's boyfriend and marry him? I'm glad you're not having tea. No time. You are leaving my house right now."

Mrs. Bell struggles to rise from the chair. Her face is so red, Sara is afraid she is going to have a heart attack before they get her off the property.

"Well," huffs Mrs. Bell. "No one will marry your daughter now." Gathering her purse from the chair, she walks out the door as fast as her short legs will transport her.

Mrs. Davis falls back in her chair and throws her arm over her eyes. Mary Ellen has not moved during this entire ordeal. She's afraid to move even now. She's never heard her gentile mother be so outspoken. Deep inside Mary Ellen, something stirs. It's a mixture of love and pride for her mother. This wonderful mixture swirls through her body. For the first time since the incident, Mary Ellen feels hope. It's going to be okay.

***

After dinner, Mrs. Davis convinces Mary Ellen to go to the mercantile store with her. "It's spring, and summer will be here before we know it. We need to buy fabric for your summer dresses, Mary Ellen, and today is a good day to do just that. Take our minds off this Thaddeus Baird mess. Sara, will you find Louis and ask him to bring the buggy around?"

"Yes, ma'am."

"Mary Ellen, run to your room and comb your hair. Let me get my hat and purse, and we'll be off."

Louis is waiting with the buggy when Mary Ellen and her mother walk out the front door of Revival House. A rather shamefaced Louis. It's the first time he has been face to face with Mrs. Davis since she heard about the incident. Louis is looking at the ground when they approach the buggy.

"Louis, look at me," says Mrs. Davis. Louis raises his head and looks at Mrs. Davis. "Don't you hang your head around me. I know all about what Thaddeus Baird did and how you saved Mary Ellen." Mrs. Davis grabs Louis' hands. "We owe you, Louis. Thank you from the bottom of our hearts. Mr. Davis feels the same way."

"Yes, ma'am. That's what Mr. Davis said. I sure feel awful."

"I know. It's a terrible thing, and we're not through facing the fallout from it. But, right now, let's go to the mercantile store and buy fabric for new dresses."

Grinning, Louis says, "Yes, ma'am."

***

Walking through the tall narrow doors of Pitts General Merchandise, Mrs. Davis spots Mrs. Pitts behind the cash register on the left side of the store, in the men's section.

"Good morning, Miss Pitts. We're just going over to the ladies' section to look at fabric for summer dresses." Mrs. Pitts nods her head at Mrs. Davis and Mary Ellen, who in turn look at each other. *Strange. Mrs. Pitts is always so friendly.* Walking over to the right side of the store to the fabric, Mary Ellen immediately spots a gleaming red silk stripped fabric.

"Mother, I love this. Can't you just see a dress out of this with a white crochet collar?"

"Maybe." Mrs. Davis pauses. "But it would be for dress-up. We need to look for light fabrics you can wear every day in the hot summer. How about this light blue cotton with the tiny white flowers?"

"Maybe," says Mary Ellen. Mary Ellen and her mother smile at each other.

"Well, you two seem to be having a good time. I can only say I'm shocked," says a tall, thin, hawk-faced woman standing in front of two other women.

"Oh, hello Mrs. Turner. And Mrs. Gray. And Mrs. Waters. How are you? I didn't hear you walk in. What were you saying?" says Mrs. Davis.

"We're shocked, Mrs. Davis." Mrs. Turner looks at Mrs. Gray and Mrs. Waters for their agreement. The two ladies quickly and grimly nod their heads up and down.

"And what shocks you?"

"You—out with your daughter in public."

"Oh, I see," says Mrs. Davis. "Mary Ellen, pick up those bolts of red silk and blue cotton and follow me to the register."

Mrs. Davis strides to the register, Mary Ellen following close behind. She is struggling to hold both bolts of cotton in her arms. Not once does Mrs. Davis look back at the ladies in the group. She waits while Mrs. Pitts cuts off five yards of fabric from each bolt, then pays the bill.

Mother and daughter walk out the door with Mary Ellen carrying the package of fabric. *So, that's how it's going to be*, Mrs. Davis thinks.

Chapter Twenty-Two
Mary Ellen Davis

Sunday May 20. 1866

Mary Ellen's mother and father are sitting in the parlor waiting for Sara to call them for supper. Mary Ellen's situation is the topic of conversation.

"You had to notice it in church this morning, Mason. Not one member of the congregation spoke to us. Not one," says Mrs. Davis

"I have noticed, Olivia. People are going out of their way to avoid us. It makes me spitting mad. The entire situation can be laid at the door of Thaddeus Baird."

"Did you write Hugh Baird?"

Getting up to pace the floor, Mr. Davis answers, "Oh, yes. I wrote him, and I tell you the fruit does not fall far from the tree. I can't believe the man who answered my letter was my old college roommate—a man I admired. Either Hugh has changed drastically or I never really knew him. He didn't believe me. Not for one second. I'm afraid we left it on bad terms. That is a friendship that has ended."

"I'm sorry to hear that, Mason. But where do we go…"

"Mr. and Mrs. Davis, you have company," says Sara, standing at the door of the parlor. "May I show Mr. Mitchell in?"

"Thomas Brown Mitchell?" asks Mrs. Davis.

"Yes, ma'am. He apologizes for coming without an invitation."

"Oh, for goodness sake. Show him in," says Mr. Davis.

Mrs. Davis stands up by her husband to greet Thomas Brown. "This is a pleasant surprise, Mr. Mitchell. May we offer you some refreshment?"

"Thank you, no." Thomas Brown, obviously nervous, is turning the brim of his hat 'round and 'round in his hands.

"Well, please be seated. I have to tell you, Mary Ellen loves working at your school almost as much as she enjoys working at the *Standard*."

"That is why I'm here. Because of Mary Ellen."

Mr. and Mrs. Davis are quiet, waiting for Thomas Brown to say more.

"I am sure Mary Ellen told you I witnessed her coming out of the old Garvey house to be followed by Mr. Baird."

"Yes."

"I've heard awful stories in town about the event, probably coming from Mrs. Bell. I'm so very sorry, and I assure you I do not in any way believe your daughter is capable of what's being said about her."

"Well, we know she did show bad judgement going in the old Garvey house. And I tell you, she sincerely regrets it," says Mr. Davis.

"I hear Mrs. Bell is telling it all over town Miss Mary Ellen will never find a husband. That is why I am here." Thomas Brown pauses. He swallows. He is trying to gather enough courage to continue.

"Mrs. Bell is wrong. I would like to request Miss Mary Ellen's hand in marriage."

Silence. The only sound is the clock ticking on the mantle.

"I'm sorry if I…"

"Please, Mr. Mitchell. You have nothing to be sorry for."

"I thought if we were engaged now, we could marry in December. My parents say an engagement must be at least six months. Ummm, that is if Mary Ellen accepts, and you approve."

"Your parents know about this?" asks Mr. Davis.

"Yes, they do. I have their full support."

"You know the gossips will talk; they are relentless. They won't stop until maybe your twentieth wedding anniversary."

"If I cared what the gossips thought, I would never be teaching sharecroppers' children at the old Garvey Plantation."

"I see your point," says Mr. Davis.

"We are humbled by your proposal, Mr. Mitchell," says Mrs. Davis, speaking for the first time. "You understand Mary Ellen will have the final say in this matter?"

"Yes, ma'am. I will not marry Miss Mary Ellen unless she chooses to marry me."

"This is a serious matter, Mr. Mitchell. I want you to have time to think over your proposal and what Mary Ellen's reputation will bring to your marriage. I want Mary Ellen to have time to give serious thought to your proposal. May we meet together here next Sunday? Will that give you enough time?"

"Yes, of course." Standing, Mr. Mitchell says, "Thank you for listening to me. And please know I do not make this offer to save Miss Mary Ellen's reputation. I have enjoyed working with her at the school and believe we could have a successful and happy life together."

Mr. Mitchell bows to Mr. and Mrs. Davis, puts his hat on his head, and walks out, leaving behind him a stunned set of parents.

***

Sara walks into the parlor, and Mr. and Mrs. Davis stand to go in to supper. Surprisingly, Sara says, "You have another visitor. Sheriff Lee is waiting on the front porch."

"Well, what now?" says Mr. Davis. "Show him in, Sara."

Sara can be heard grumbling. How is she going to get supper ready if people keep coming to the Revival House?

The sheriff walks in the parlor, hat in hand. "Sorry to disturb you folks on a Sunday afternoon."

"Don't fash, Bobby. No problem. How have you been, and how's your mother?"

"She's fine, Mrs. Davis. Still has arthritis. I'll tell her you asked about her."

"How can we help you, Bobby?" says Mr. Davis

"Well, I won't deny this is awkward, so I'm going to ask you right out. Have you seen Thaddeus Baird recently? He hasn't been seen since May 11th."

"May 11th?" says Mrs. Davis. She and Mr. Davis look at each other. It connects. That's the day Thaddeus attacked Mary Ellen.

"No, we haven't. And it is a good thing, I tell you," says Mr. Davis.

Sheriff Lee looks down at the floor, embarrassed.

"I'm sure you are hearing stories about Mary Ellen," Mr. Davis says. "The real story is Thaddeus attacked her in the old Garvey house, and Louis saved her. We know Mary

Ellen should not have gone in the house alone, but, my God, Baird attacked her."

"That's one of the stories I heard," says the sheriff.

"You say Thaddeus has disappeared?" asks Mrs. Davis.

"Seems to be right. His father came by my office yesterday because he can't get in touch with Thaddeus."

"Yes, I'm sure his father does want to get in touch with him. Hugo Baird and I were college roommates. Of course, I wrote him about what happened. I'm afraid he denied his son would do such a thing."

"Well, it is an odd thing. Not one soul on Howard College has seen him since supper at the college cafeteria on that Friday night. You can see why his father is concerned."

"Yes, it is odd, for sure. You know, I think Revival House would be the last place on earth he would visit," says Mr. Davis.

"I agree with you, but had to check. I'll see myself out. I heard Sara grumbling about not getting supper ready because of visitors." Sheriff Lee smiles. "I don't want to keep you from your supper."

"You are welcome to stay and eat with us," says Mrs. Davis.

"Thank you for the kind invitation, but I have to get back to my office. Please let me know if you hear from Thaddeus Baird."

"I will, Sheriff. And have a nice evening," says Mr. Davis.

Waiting until he sees Sheriff Lee walk down the porch steps and ride off on his horse, Mr. Davis yells, "Sara, are there any more visitors out on the porch?"

Sara appears in the door. "Mr. and Mrs. Davis, you can come to supper now."

Chapter Twenty-Three
Ellen Jones

Sunday, April 1, 1962

Sunday afternoon finds Ellen and a much-improved Essie searching in the parlor for the secret drawer Lottie mentioned. The two have already covered the bedrooms upstairs, with no success. After a short lemonade break on the veranda, they move on to the parlor and dining room.

Ellen looks over the familiar room with its two tufted Victorian sofas facing each other, their ornate feet sitting atop an intricate design on the oriental rug. Two chairs separated by a pie crust table complete the grouping of furniture. A fireplace with mantle and painting above, plus a large secretary desk, line the far wall past the sofa and chairs. On the wall nearest the door are the mint julep cabinet and matching secretary.

"You just know that secret drawer is in this room. We should have started here first," says Essie.

"Now, Aunt Essie, we agreed Mary Ellen would have access to a secret drawer in her bedroom. So much more private that way."

"But we didn't find one, did we, Ellen?" Pause. "Listen to me. I am so cranky. It was being in that hospital. I'm sorry, Ellen."

Ellen walks to Essie and gently enfolds Essie in her arms. "I love you, Aunt Essie. You just crank away if it makes you feel better."

"Well, it doesn't. It makes me feel like a sour lemon. I promise to be better. Now, I'll take the pie crust table if you'll take the mint julep cabinet."

Moving to the table, Essie asks, "You know why this round table is called a pie crust table?"

"No," says Ellen rather cheekily, "But you will give me the fascinating history, I'm sure."

"Well, smarty pants, it is called that because it resembles a pie crust with its crimped edges."

"Oh," says Ellen, as she gets on her knees to search the mint julep cabinet. After close exploration of both pieces—knobs turned, buttons pushed, drawers explored—the two have no luck.

"Let's move on to the secretaries. We are going to have to be more creative. Turn everything that can turn," says Essie.

"And push," says Ellen. "See these panels above each mail slot on the secretaries? I'm going to push each one." With a push of the third small panel, Ellen shrieks. A drawer slides forward with a cavity just large enough to hold jewelry or a letter. This drawer is empty. But when Ellen pushes on the next panel, she meets with success. There are pages crumbled to fit the drawer.

"Essie, I've got it!"

Essie joins Ellen and the two extract the pages from the drawer. Ellen carefully smooths the first page out. Looking at the bottom, she sees the notation: *Mary Ellen Davis.*

"It looks like a journal entry. Let's sit on the sofa and read it together."

***

Stupid! Stupid! Stupid!

Why did I follow Thaddeus Baird into the old Garvey house? I knew better. Mother has drilled into me: never be alone in a room—much less a moldy plantation house—with a man.

It seemed romantic at the time. Poor Louis. I made him stay on the wagon. Stupid!

Even when Thaddeus offered me the ring, I felt uneasy. Knew something was off. But what a ring it was—gold with three sapphires.

He attacked me. I can't get the picture of him ripping my blouse off my mind.

Wonderful Louis! What would I have done if he hadn't saved me?

Oh, and Mrs. Bell. Of all people, why did she have to be the one to see me running out of the house?

And Thomas Brown. It breaks my heart. He saw it all. What must he think of me?

Got to go. I hear Mother calling. My heart will be broken forever.

Mary Ellen Davis
Saturday, May 12, 1866

***

There was a second journal entry—and a third. Ellen read each entry aloud as Aunt Essie sat in rapt attention.

*Over dinner tonight, Father tells me
Thomas Brown Mitchell has asked for my hand
in marriage.*

*How can that be? He knows about what
happened with Thaddeus Baird. Why would he
want to marry me?*

*Mary Ellen Davis
Sunday, May 20, 1866*

***

*Someone, probably one of my aunts,
once advised me to marry a good, kind man—
a religious man who is an achiever. A man to
respect. Love. That mysterious word. Love will
come later, after living together day by day.
After sharing the horrors life sends your way.
And the thrilling times as well. I think Thomas
Brown Mitchell is such a man.*

Could I love him?

*I feel horrible beyond belief over what my
parents are going through because of my
behavior. I am accepting Thomas Brown mainly*

because of them, but I am accepting him for me
as well. Thomas Brown and I have the same
interests. I can see myself working side by side
with him. I can see myself sharing a home with
him. Could I love him?

My Lord! My life has changed, but you are
with me. I think you will bless this marriage.

Oh, one more thing. Sheriff Lee came by.
Thaddeus Baird is missing. I hope they don't
find him for a hundred years.

Mary Ellen Davis
Wednesday, May 23, 1866

***

Just as Essie and Ellen read the last journal entry, the
telephone rings. "You sit, Aunt Essie. I'll get it." Ellen gets
up from the floor and walks toward the kitchen to answer
the phone.

Essie can hear Ellen talking over the telephone, but she
can't hear what she is saying. *Probably someone bringing*
over dinner. My, but these Marshall people are wonderful.
Essie rests her head on the back of the sofa and closes her
eyes. But not for long.

"Essie, wake up. You really will not believe this! That was Dad. They have found a body in a tunnel at the old Garvey plantation house. From all appearances, it is a man. Looks like he's been there a long while."

Essie sits straight up. She and Ellen stare at each other. They say the name simultaneously: "Thaddeus Baird."

Chapter Twenty-Four
Mary Ellen Davis

Monday, May 21, 1866

Sara, alone at Revival House, is in the kitchen washing up after breakfast when she hears a knock on the kitchen door. Opening the door, Sara finds Louis on the porch. Sara hasn't seen Louis since Friday, the day Mary Ellen was attacked. She was glad to hear from Mary Ellen that Louis was not punished for his role in the event, and it's a relief to see his face this morning.

"Louis, good morning. Come in this kitchen. Do you want some coffee? There's some left from breakfast."

"Yes, ma'am," says Louis, walking in the kitchen.

"Well, sit down then. I'll have a cup with you."

After getting his coffee, Louis adds sugar and stirs and stirs.

"Louis, you're gonna rub the sides off that coffee cup. What's wrong with you?"

Louis stops stirring and looks up. "I've done a horrible thing, Sara. I'm scared to death somebody gonna find out."

"Louis, it can't be that bad. You wanna tell me about it?"

"Yes, ma'am. But you gotta promise to not tell one solitary soul."

"I think I can promise that. Now, what did you do?"

"I killed Thaddeus Baird."

Sara, open-jawed, just stares at him.

"Did you hear what I said?" asks Louis.

"I did, and I think you better explain."

"I never liked the man from the first day I saw him. Remember the Sunday he first came for dinner? I was outside when he pulled up in his buggy. Right away he asked me if I was the Davis' nigger. You know Mr. Davis would have had a fit if he'd heard that word. You know that word is not used around Revival House."

"What did you do, Louis?" asks Sara.

"I turned my back on him and walked to the back of the house."

"I mean now... You, you killed him? My thoughts on Mr. Baird are exactly the same as yours, but I wouldn't kill him. What happened, Louis?"

"I set out to punish the man, so I went to Marion, to that college. I saw him come out of a building on campus and get on his horse. I was riding Bonnie, so I followed him. He rode to the Garvey plantation and went inside the old plantation house. I could see him through one of the windows. He was on his hands and knees looking for something, and he finally found what he was looking for—the ring he tried to give Miss Mary Ellen."

"The pre-engagement ring," says Sara, with a sneer.

"That's the one."

"So, what happened?"

"He was surprised to see me at first, then he smiled and said he was real glad I showed up. He said I had something coming to me for breaking up him and Miss Mary Ellen."

"Oh, Louis."

"That man came at me with murder in his eye. He grabbed me around the throat, and I swear, I thought I was gonna die."

"But you didn't."

"No. I grabbed my hunting knife out of my boot and stabbed him in the gut. I only meant to stop him. I tell you —it was the worst moment of my life."

"So, what did you do? You didn't just walk off and leave him, did you?"

"No. I just sat on the ground thinking while Mr. Baird was dying. Then I remembered the tunnel."

"What tunnel?"

"When I was a kid, my friends and I played in and around the old Garvey House. My grandpa told me there was a tunnel from the house to the kitchen, so the slaves could bring the food from the kitchen to the dining room without going outside. My friends and I found the tunnel and played in it."

"I've never heard of such."

"Well, thank goodness for Grandpa telling me about the tunnel because that's exactly where I put Thaddeus Baird's body. The ring with the three stones was on his little finger. I left it there."

"But Louis, won't your friends remember the tunnel if anything ever comes up about the old Garvey House."

"Most of them have moved to Mobile. And who's gonna think to even search for Thaddeus Baird in the old Garvey house?"

"You're probably right. Now, listen to me, Louis. You can't tell anyone about this. And I'll take the story to my grave. Do you hear me?"

"Yes, ma'am. Don't you worry. I'm too scared to tell anybody."

"And, Louis.... I hope you don't spend one more minute thinking about that man. You've got to put this behind you —for Miss Mary Ellen, for all of us.."

"Honestly, I think I'll see the look on his face while he choked me for the rest of my life. Thy shall not kill. I hope God forgives me."

Chapter Twenty-Five
Ellen Jones

Friday, April 6. 1962

Ellen is in her dorm room, sitting on the bed with her shoes off, legs crossed. There are two envelopes on the bed beside her. One letter is from Jo Jo; the other appears to be an invitation with Mr. Chenard's name in the return address. Curious, Ellen opens the envelope and pulls out the invitation.

Please join us to celebrate
Louisa's arrival in the United States

A Black-Tie Dinner
Thursday, April twelfth
One thousand nine hundred sixty-two

six o'clock in the evening
The Camilla Room
1000 Anastasia Avenue
Miami, Florida

R.S.V.P. by April tenth
1 (855) 311-5444

She made it. Mr. Chenard has his Louisa with him in Miami. Ellen notices another piece of paper in the envelope. Pulling the paper out, she finds a handwritten note from Mr. Chenard: "Bring a friend with you." Ellen will have to think about Mr. Chenard's request.

Opening the letter from Jo Jo, Ellen checks first to make sure the phrase "You're still my girl," is there at the conclusion of the letter. It is. Smiling, she starts to read:

Dear Ellen,

I know what I want to do with my life. I want to work for the United States Department of Agriculture in the Foreign Affairs Agency. That's a mouthful, isn't it?

You know I have fallen in love with Libya. I told you I feel I'm walking where the ancients walked. There's that aspect of the country; the other aspect of the country is the poverty.

I feel I could help with food availability in developing nations. I have the background— growing up on Callander and working with your dad. But I don't have the education. I need a master's degree to work with the Department of Agriculture. So, that is my plan. I can get my degree while serving in the Air Force.

I have already enrolled in two courses through the University of Maryland. Us airmen are lucky to have the University offering courses in foreign lands, and the University offers counseling here at the base as to degree requirements. So, I'm off and running.

Just so you know, I want you on this journey. I think of us traveling the world—you creating wonderful documentaries and me helping other nations.

I wrote you a poem. I know you still have it. Remember the first two lines:

I feel that I can aim high.
I never feel that I am just a sharecropper's son.

We can aim high together, Ellen. We have a lot to talk about when I come home this summer.

You're still my girl,
Jo Jo

Ellen slowly folds the letter and places it back in its envelope. She remembers Luella's third prediction: *She will find the soldier.* But she had found more than one. Jonas Stockman, the Revolutionary War soldier buried on Callander land, was the first soldier. Thomas Brown Mitchell was a Civil War soldier. That's two. And Jo Jo Reed is in the Air Force. Three Soldiers.

Did Luella's prediction mean she will marry Jo Jo?

A little stunned by her thought, Ellen thinks about a future with Jo Jo. Imagine living in other countries spread out across the world. The stories she could write. The images she could capture. The idea takes her breath away.

See Ellen's Notebook for Jo Jo's complete poem.

***

Glancing down, Ellen spots Mr. Chenard's invitation and sees his enclosed note again: *Bring someone.* It hits her that Jack Marin would be the perfect person to bring to Mr. Chenard's party. Standing up and wriggling her feet into her shoes, Ellen heads for the broadcasting studio to extend an invitation. She's lucky and finds Jack in the studio working on a script.

"I thought you left a long time ago," says Jack.

"I did, but I came back to ask you a question," says Ellen.

"Fire away."

"My wonderful Cuban friend, Mr. Chenard, is hosting a black-tie affair on Thursday, April 12th, in celebration of Louisa escaping Cuba to join him. As you can guess, Louisa is his wife. I received an invitation with instructions to bring someone. He is a lovely man, and I would like for you two to meet. What do you say? Are you up for an elegant affair, Jack?"

"Is that your way of asking me if I have a tux? I assure you, I do."

"No," laughs Ellen. "I just think you two would be fast friends. I'd like to be the one to introduce you two."

"Well, in that case, it is my honor to go with you."

"Thank you, Jack. We'll work out the details later"

"Thank you, director lady. I look forward to it."

Chapter Twenty-Six
Ellen Jones

Thursday, April 12, 1962

Walking into the restaurant, Ellen breathes in the air of Cuba. Cigar smoke. Rum. The fragrance of White Mariposas. Handsome men in tuxedos and women in long flowing gowns are conversing in groups with the music of Celia Cruz playing in the background.

Ellen's attention is riveted toward the restaurant's dance floor. Mr. Chenard and a very feminine lady with dark hair drawn into a chignon, forming a knot at the back of her neck, are dancing. Her skin is olive, and her eyes are emerald green. She follows Mr. Chenard effortlessly. They dance as one. When the music ends, Mr. Chenard takes Louisa by the hand and brings her to Ellen and Jack.

"Louisa, I want you to meet Ellen, our American daughter."

Ellen swallows, trying to rid her throat of the hard knot that forms when she is emotional.

"Ellen," says Louisa, "I owe you a debt for being a part of Juan David's life here in Miami. It is such a pleasure to meet you."

"The pleasure is mine, Louisa. I have heard so much about you and your life in Cuba. How wonderful that you are here."

Taking Mr. Chenard's arm, Louisa says, "Yes, my life in Cuba." Louisa looks reflective and sad.

"But she is with us now. Nothing but love, good Cuban food, and life ahead of us," says Mr. Chenard.

Jack has been silently standing, watching the interaction between the three. Turning around, Ellen pulls him forward.

"Ah, I see you did honor my request. You brought a young man."

"Louisa and Mr. Chenard, I am pleased to introduce you to a new broadcasting student, Jack Marin. He has ties to Cuba, and I know you two will enjoy getting to know each other."

Louisa smiles graciously, and Mr. Chenard extends his hand. "Are you related to Ernesto Marin?"

Jack nods. "He is my father."

"A fine man. Then I do look forward to talking with you. Thank you for coming, Jack. Make Ellen bring you to the police station so we can talk soon. And now, I'm being signaled. It is time to find our seats for dinner. Ellen, you are at a table near the front. Oh, and I expect a dance from you after dinner."

As Mr. Chenard and Louisa walk away, Jack asks, "The police station?"

"Come. Let's find our seats, and I will explain Mr. Chenard to you."

As Mr. Chenard indicated, Ellen and Jack find their places at a table near the front of the restaurant. The handwritten place cards indicate "Ellen Jones" on both cards. As soon as they are seated, an appetizer of toasted walnuts, lemon, and sage is placed in front of them.

"The police station?" asks Jack.

"Mr. Chenard is a janitor at the police station. I met him for the first time when I went to interview one of the detectives. I was stuck by the elegance of the man with a trash can in his hands."

"Why the police station?"

"The only employment Mr. Chenard could find. It is temporary, I assure you. Mr. Chenard taught literature at the University of Havana. He was also very anti-Castro, as Castro dictated that Mr. Chenard and others could only teach Marxist literature in their classes."

"Is that why he left Cuba?" asks Jack.

"Partially. Mr. Chenard became active politically. Oddly, he wrote a song about freedom that Cubans still sing in the streets. As Louisa's family is close to the president of Cuba,

Mr. Chenard felt he had to leave Cuba to protect her. Had his anti-Castro activities become uncovered, Louisa would have suffered gravely."

"You said his job at the police station is temporary?"

"I think so. Mr. Chenard is taking classes to be certified as a teacher in the United States. I think he'll leave the trash can behind as soon as he gets his degree."

At that point in their conversation the appetizer plate is replaced by a plate of pan roasted chicken breasts served with goat cheese, grits, arugula, and gremolata, an Italian condiment.

"I think Mr. Chenard is introducing Louisa to a cuisine that is not Cuban."

"Fine by me," says Jack, as he deftly slices the chicken breasts. After a moment, he asks, "Ellen, I know about your story with Luke. That is your past, and I'm more interested in your future. I would love to get to know you, so I am just going to ask. Do you have someone in your life?"

Ellen is touched. She likes Jack Marin. She pauses and then answers directly. "I do, Jack. It's a boy from home. We grew up together. He wants to work for the Department of Agriculture and travel the world. He wants me to travel with him."

"And is that something you want?"

"I think it is, Jack."

Mr. Chenard taps Ellen on the shoulder. "May I have this dance?"

Ellen smiles at Mr. Chenard, remembering the first time they danced together. It was a Mambo. Mr. Chenard had invited Ellen to a Cuban party. When Ellen and Mr. Chenard took to the floor, everyone else moved back. They realized something special was happening. Ellen had not danced the Mambo before that night, but she threw herself into the dance. She felt creative. She felt free. When the last note of the song faded, the beautiful Cubans in the room applauded Ellen and Mr. Chenard. Not an experience she would forget.

Once again, Ellen and Mr. Chenard dance to "Mucho, Mucho, Mucho." During the dance, Mr. Chenard asks, "Now, Ellen, is this young man important to you?"

Ellen throws her head back and laughs. "I just met him. He left his old university and came to Columbus. He is majoring in broadcast journalism. He's anchoring our show."

"Just like Luke, right?"

"No, not just like Luke. He does not have Luke's ego, and Jack's not a part of my life in that way."

"And that boy back home?"

"Jo Jo." She smiles. "Yes, he is a part of my life."

Mr. Chenard swings Ellen around at the end of the dance. "I expect to meet this Jo Jo."

"I will make that happen. And now, if I am reading him right, my escort is ready to leave."

Mr. Chenard leads Ellen to Louisa. He and Louisa hug Ellen and thank her for coming.

"Louisa, I see you are exactly where you belong. I am so happy for you both."

Louisa replies, "I look forward to many hours getting to know you, Ellen."

Ellen smiles at this beautiful Cuban lady. "That will happen, Louisa. We will make sure it does."

Ellen and Jack ride back to campus in a cab. Both are lost in thought. Arriving at Ellen's dorm, Jack walks Ellen to the door.

"Thank you for asking me, Ellen. It was a special night."

Before Ellen can protest, Jack leans in and kisses her on the lips.

Chapter Twenty-Seven
Ellen Jones

Saturday, April 14, 1962

Ellen is sleeping late when she hears the telephone in the dorm hall ringing. Again. Turning over, she ignores it, hoping it will stop ringing. *Yes.* It does. Silence. *No, now it's ringing again.* Grumbling, Ellen stumbles out of bed and makes her way down the hall to the old telephone booth.

Picking up the phone, Ellen hears Essie talking a mile a minute almost before she can say hello. "Whoa, Aunt Essie. I'm just waking up. You are going to have to repeat that."

"Oh, sorry Ellen. But I had to tell you right away. It's in the paper. That body found in the tunnel in the old Garvey plantation house? There was a ring on one of the fingers. A gold ring set with three sapphires. How about that?"

"Then the body is Thaddeus Baird, for sure. But what does finding his body solve the mystery of what happened?" says Ellen.

"He probably has relatives who would like to know what happened to the man. But you are right. Nothing is solved. We'll never know why his body was in the tunnel."

"Well, Essie, I say he got his just rewards."

"Do not be deceived. God cannot be mocked. A man reaps what he sows. Galatians 6:7."

"You are correct, Essie."

"Now, there's more news. I pushed on the rest of those panels on the secretary where you were searching. And guess what?"

"What?"

"I found a newspaper article dated in 1892. It was all about the success of the Jericho School. Mary Ellen and Thomas Brown added a dormitory behind the old plantation house, so children outside the area could come to school. They built onto the school, to house more children, and they added several teachers."

"That's wonderful news, Essie. I just bet they had a happy marriage, too. I'm so glad."

"Yes, it warms my heart."

"Mine, too," says Ellen.

"I do have some other news. Nick is joining the family for Sunday dinner."

"Nick?" says Ellen.

"Nicholas Ellard, you goose."

"Oh, yes. The tall, dark, 'absolutely gorgeous' man."

"Yes, that's the one," says Essie, chuckling.

"I could reach through the telephone line and hug you. I am so happy for you."

"And what's your news? I want to be happy for you, too."

"Well, I'll just say that Old Luella's third prediction is coming true."

Chapter Twenty-Eight
Ellen Jones

Friday, June 1, 1962

Ellen has been waiting in the Mobile airport for over an hour now. She's waiting for Jo Jo to disembark from his flight home from Tripoli. The flight has landed, and the attendants are pushing the mobile staircase to the plane's door, which has just opened. People begin to disembark and stream through the doors onto the hot runway.

A businessman in a tan suit, briefcase in hand, comes off first. He is followed by a harried young woman dragging two small, very unhappy children. Then: *Jo Jo.* Even from a distance Ellen would recognize handsome Jo Jo with his square jaw and dimple that shows when he smiles.

She makes her way across the tarmac toward him. Ellen is waiting at the bottom of the staircase when he reaches the last step. "There's my girl," says Jo Jo. He opens his arms and Ellen steps in, places her arms around his body and squeezes him tight, as if to anchor him to this time and place. She knows it's a moment she will treasure forever.

Ellen looks up into Jo Jo's face. He moves his mouth down to hers. At last, he is home. Breaking apart from Ellen, Jo Jo asks, "Ellen Jones, would you like to see the world with me?"

"Why, yes I would," says Ellen.

"That means you have to marry me."

"I would think so." Pausing for a moment, Ellen looks at Jo Jo and says, "I love you."

Chapter Twenty-Nine
Mary Ellen Davis

Friday, June 1, 1866

School is over for the day, and Benjamin and Ruth are the last to leave the kitchen turned school house. After they leave, Mary Ellen is busy straightening the books that are all tumbled together on the shelves beneath the windows.

"Leave those Mary Ellen, and come sit with me," says Thomas Brown, as he sits down in one of the tufted armchairs at the front of the room.

Propping up one last book, *Treasure Island* by Robert Louis Stevenson, Mary Ellen stands up and walks to the other armchair. Sitting down, she says, "I love seeing books all tumbled about. It means they are being searched through by a child looking for a good read."

"Yes, but once and a while they need to be set right," says Thomas Brown. "Just like some of the people in this town."

"Oh, you can't imagine how hard this whole Thaddeus Baird situation has been. I was very foolish."

"No, you were an innocent, and he is a true scoundrel."

"The thing that hurts most is the way people have treated my parents. How can they be so cruel?"

"It may seem the whole town is against you, but I know for a fact that is not true. My parents are not, and none of their friends are. As a matter of fact, Mary Ellen, my parents are very excited about a wedding in the family."

"I am amazed at their reaction—and yours, too. Are you sure you want to marry me?"

"I have wanted to marry you since you first walked through the school house door."

"You have?"

"Of course, Mary Ellen. Who wouldn't want to marry you? You are bright. You have a beautiful soul. You love children. And you have wonderful visions for the future."

"I've been thinking since last Sunday when my parents accepted your proposal. I do have visions for the future... for our future. We can work miracles together at Jericho School. We can expand, hire more teachers, send these wonderful children to college."

"Yes, Mary Ellen. We can do all that. And just think about our own children."

Blushing, Mary Ellen looks down at her hands.

"Look at me, Mary Ellen. Our children will be leaders. They will be lawyers, educators, and a few just have to be journalists." Thomas Brown smiles at his last remark.

"We are about to have our first argument. More than just a few will be journalists."

"If you say so, Mary Ellen." Thomas Brown picks up Mary Ellen's hand and gently kisses the palm. Mary Ellen looks at the crown of his head as the bends over her hand. This is a man who fought in the Civil War and returned wounded. And what did he do? He chose to help children rise above a life of poverty. This is a man Mary Ellen can spend her life with.

Mary Ellen smiles at Thomas Brown as he lifts his head. "My prediction? We have a beautiful future ahead."

Epilogue

Sunday, October 16, 1966

Sitting down on my bed,
I reach for a baby book lying on the bedside table.

I open the satin cover and begin filling in
memories of our first days together.

It is for my daughter.

Born seven days ago, on October 9, 1966,
her name is Zia Louise Reed.

I wonder what Luella will predict for her.

Ellen's
Notebook

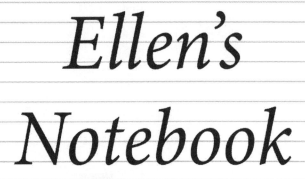
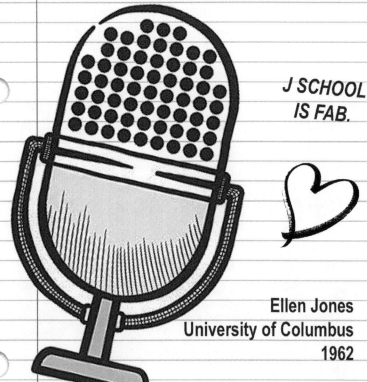

J SCHOOL
IS FAB.

Ellen Jones
University of Columbus
1962

The Garvey Plantation Kitchen

Kitchens in the Old South were often outdoor buildings. Cooking was done on wood-burning stoves and open hearths, causing a lot of heat to be released into the kitchen area. The outdoor kitchen kept the heat plus smells away from the main house.

Thomas Brown Mitchell was related to the Garveys of Garvey plantation through his mother, whose Aunt Ivy married Andrew Garvey. Andrew and Ivy had no children, and when they both died in 1856, the home was left to ruin.

Essie found this picture of the Garvey Kitchen, which became the Jericho School, in the tall desk or secretary located in the front parlor of the Mitchell House.

Jo Jo in Gus Grissom's flight suit.

Gus Grissom, the second astronaut in space, piloted the second Project Mercury flight. The spacecraft was named Liberty Bell 7 and was launched from Cape Canaveral, Florida. The flight lasted fifteen minutes and thirty-seven seconds.

Gus Grissom was a veteran of World War II and the Korean War. Besides piloting Liberty Bell 7, he was command pilot on the first manned Gemini flight and also served as command pilot for the first three-man Apollo flight, Apollo 1. The purpose of the Apollo missions was to land the first man on the moon. Unfortunately, a flash fire occurred in Apollo 1, killing Gus Grissom and the other two astronauts.

"Photographer Jackie Kennedy"

Miami News Now / Ellen Jones / March 27, 1962

Suggested anchor lead-in	Before she was our most-photographed first lady, Jackie Kennedy was behind the camera. Here's Ellen Jones with the story.
Shot of Jackie with camera	VO… The beautiful, young photographer could be any photographer on the streets of New York. Stylish but professional black dress, short bobbed hair, camera with flash attachment held at the ready.
Shot of Jackie in front of White House	VO… What sets this photographer apart is… she is Jacqueline Bouvier, destined to be first lady of the United States.
Shot of interview scene in Washington D.C.	VO… When Bouvier graduated from George Washington University in 1951, *The Washington Times Herald* hired her to interview and photograph people on the streets. Bouvier wrote an ongoing series of articles based on her interviews.
Shot of newspaper column	VO… Her articles were titled "The Inquiring Camera Girl" and the format consisted of a question followed by an answer with photograph of the interviewee.
Coronation of Queen Elizabeth	VO… One assignment involved Bouvier being sent to London for Queen Elizabeth's coronation. She asked people in the crowd outside Buckingham Palace, "Do you think Queen Elizabeth will be your last queen?"
Shot of Kennedy in the senate	VO… In April 1953, she interviewed the young United States senator from Massachusetts, John F. Kennedy, and his high-school-aged page or aide. The question posed: "What is it like observing each other at close range?" Kennedy responded that the country might be better off if the senators and their pages traded places.
Jerry Hoobler, page for Senator John F. Kennedy	SOT… Senator Kennedy is often taken for a tourist by the capitol police because he is so young. The other day an officer told the senator that the special phones were reserved for senators.
Shot of Kennedy wedding	VO… Bouvier held her job with the *Times-Herald* for two years. Just months after she resigned from the *Herald*, she married John F. Kennedy on September 12, 1953.
Ellen Jones *Miami News Now*	How interesting to know… our first lady was one of us. Holding a camera. Asking interview questions. Writing the story.

Writing a feature story

What is a feature story and how does it differ from a hard news story? Hard news stories are time-sensitive and often cover breaking news. Feature stories are more in-depth and are usually evergreen, meaning they are not time sensitive. News stories focus on events where feature stories are more apt to focus on the people involved in the event.

The Lead

Whereas the lead in a hards news story begins with who, what, where, when, and sometimes why and how, a feature story lead involves revealing the story more slowly. Feature stories may begin by setting the scene or telling a story. In the feature lead below, see the difference between a hard news opening and the opening paragraph below that sets the scene.

Hard News Lead

The Washington Times-Herald hired Jacqueline Bouvier in 1951 to produce a series of articles titled "The Inquiring Camera Girl."

Feature Lead

The beautiful, young photographer could be any photographer on the streets of New York. Sytylish but professional black dress, short bobbed hair, camera with flash attachment at the ready. What sets this photographer apart? She is Jacqueline Bovier, destined to be first lady of the United States.

The Body

In the body of the story, the reader learns the details of the story. The body of the story includes events, quotes from people related to the story, and other information that supports the lead. The information in the story about Jacqueline Bouvier is conveyed in chronological order. This is often the case in a feature story, but any logical order will do.

In the Jacqueline Bouvier story, the reader learns that Bouvier was the Inquiring Camera girl. She was sent to London for Queen Elizabeth's coronation, and she interviewed the young senator, John F. Kennedy.

Conclusion

Make your final point about the subject in the conclusion. You may refer back to the lead by recapping the main focus of your story.

How interesting to know...our first lady was one of us. Holding a camera. Asking interview questions. Writing the story.

Scriptwriting Using a Split-Page Format

Aunt Zia says, "Remember the viewer is hearing and seeing
the story. You have to plan in advance and explain what the viewer
is seeing as you report the news.."

Stories for television are written in a split-page format. Video
is described on the left, and audio narrative is written on the
right.

Video Instructions

VO

VO stands for Voiceover, which means the viewer hears
the reporter or anchor, but on the screen the viewer sees
footage that supports what the reporter or anchor is saying.
Throughout the Jackie Bouvier story, the audience
hears the reporter but sees footage. VO footage seen in the
Jackie Bouvier story includes the Coronation of Queen
Elizabeth, the wedding of the Kennedys, and Jackie Bouvier in
front of the White House.

SOT

SOT stands for Sound on Tape, which means a sound bite or
brief excerpt from a recording, such as a complete interview.
In the Bouvier story, there is a SOT from Kennedy's page,
Jerry Hoobler.

VO/Sot

SOTs need to be brief. You may start a portion of the script
as an SOT and then add footage that complements the
SOT. That is a VO/SOT.

"Leaving Callander"

By
Jo Jo Reed

I feel that I can aim high.
I never feel that I am just a sharecropper's son.

People say we live in a two-room shack.
My parents never say we are poor.

I believe I am an achiever and will travel far.
No one believes I will see the world beyond Alabama.

I have lived on Callander land, and I know
every inch by smell, taste, touch.
I know I could leave if you went with me.

My friends say you will never look at me.
I believe we could live together forever
anywhere.

Ellen's Family Tree

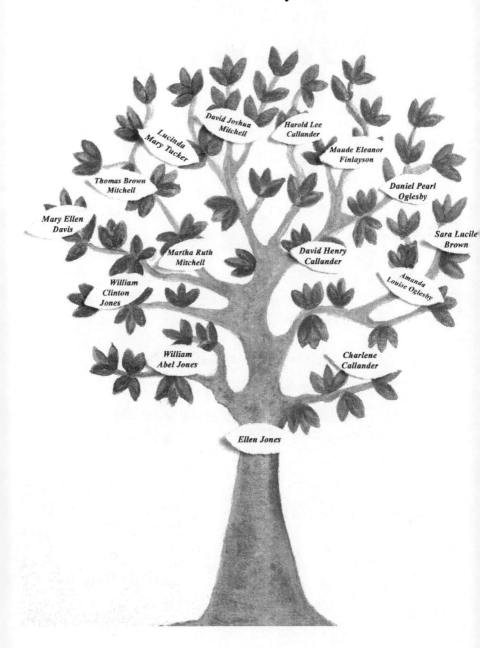

Acknowledgements

I was fortunate to grow up near Marion, Alabama—home of gracious people and stunning antebellum homes. While staying in one of those homes, I was introduced to a mint julep cabinet with carving on the back panel. Years later, I remember the cabinet and thought of the role it could play in this mystery.

Callander plantation is based on my grandfather's home where he and his wife raised ten children. The grist mill, commissary, syrup mill, sawmill, blacksmith shop, cotton gin and 1,200 acres of rich farmland described in my Ellen books all really existed. Revolutionary War soldier, George Mayberry, is buried on this land, and he is the inspiration for Jonas Stockman in my Ellen novels.

The shelter built for President Kennedy would have been a secret at the time Ellen delivered it as a news story. Apologies for not sticking to the correct timeline.

Thank you to the wonderfully creative Dawn Richerson for her involvement in the editing and publishing of *A Mystery Solved, A Prediction Fulfilled.* Dawn has been involved in the publishing of all four of my books, and I'm so sure they would not have seen the light of day without her.

Thank you to Beta readers Becky Lester, Patti Twombly, Karen West, and my husband, L.C. I appreciate you and can't thank you enough for catching the errors I made in the telling of the story.

Susan Sikes Davis, who owns the fabulous shop, Sikes and Davis, in downtown Lawrenceville, has hosted two book launches for the Ellen books. I am so grateful for her generosity and love just being around this extremely creative lady.

Hugs, love, and deepest gratitude to the beautiful friends in my life. I am stunned by the ways you support me as an author and a friend.

My husband, L.C., has supported my author's journey in ways too numerous to count. He can hawk my books in ways that continue to amaze me. Love and gratitude, L.C.

I am so thankful to be a part of the Jones and Smith families. Yes, I was a Jones and married a Smith. And I am thankful everyday for our children Doug, Christy, Jeff, and Katie.

About the Author

Alayne Smith is a retired broadcast journalism teacher who earned M. Ed. and Ed. S. degrees in Instructional Technology from the University of Georgia. She taught for over twenty-five years in Gwinnett County, Ga., where she developed the first broadcast journalism course at the high school level. With other Gwinnett County broadcast journalism teachers, she contributed to the development of an eight-course continuum of courses in broadcast journalism and video production. She was Bell South Teacher of the Year and in 2003 was Brookwood High School's Teacher of the Year. She served as a committee member for the International Student Media Festival, 1995-1998, and as a CNN Student Bureau Advisor, 1999-2001.

Ellen and the Three Predictions, published in March 2017 by Cactus Moon Publications, is a historical fiction novel written for young adults and Alayne's first novel. Set in the late 1950s and early 1960s, *Ellen and the Three Predictions* details the life of an aspiring broadcast journalist, Ellen Jones, and the predictions made for Ellen's life by Old Luella, a local soothsayer.

Educating Sadie, published in August 2019, was a finalist in the 2018 William Faulkner – William Wisdom Creative Writing Competition. *Educating Sadie* follows one woman's struggle to help another woman rise above a life of poverty and abuse in nineteenth-century Alabama. Amanda Oglesby is a first-year teacher who meets Sadie Wiggins, a sharecropper's wife, on the night of the first open house at her new school. Childless, Sadie is drawn to the school: she's bright and wants to learn. The relationship develops when Amanda invites Sadie to attend daily school classes. A benevolent school board chairman, a beloved boarding house owner, a midwife, a handsome plantation owner, and a misanthrope move in the background of *Educating Sadie,* a portrait of the American South at the turn of the century.

Alayne's third novel, *This Is Ellen Jones Reporting*, follows the story of Ellen Jones as she follows her dream of becoming a broadcast journalist. Set in 1961, this sequel to *Ellen and the Three Predictions* draws on the developing stories of Luke and Ellen with glimpses of her beloved Callander and college life as they pursue their degrees. Again, Cuba is a thread in Smith's novels as Zia works on a documentary about the real events at the Bay of Pigs and Ellen competes for a Peabody Award with her story of a former literature teacher at the University of Havana who was forced to leave the Cuba he loves.

Alayne is a member of the Atlanta Writers Club, the Georgia Association for Instructional Technology, the Georgia Writers Association, the Southeastern Writers Association, and the Society of Children's Book Writers and Illustrators. She currently lives in Lawrenceville, Georgia, with her husband. Follow Alayne at http://alaynesmith.com.

Made in United States
Orlando, FL
03 January 2024